COWBOY'S ACCIDENTAL WIFE

J.P. COMEAU

Boone

"One. Two. Three. Four. Fi—shit, come on. Five. Six. Seven. Oh, yeah. Argh."

I brought the bar of weights down to my waist before dropping them to the soaked mat beneath my feet. I threaded my fingers together and laced them above my head, opening my lungs as I breathed deeply, inhaling the salty air. I closed my eyes and took a step back, lunging so I could stretch out my muscles.

And when I opened my eyes, I found myself staring into a wall-to-wall mirror in front of me.

While all sorts of thoughts still tumbled around in my mind.

"Fuck," I groaned.

My weakened arms fell to my sides as I tilted back my head. I rolled it around from side to side until my neck cracked, relieving the pressure that had been building at the base of my skull. There were so many changes that had taken place in my family over the past few years, and it had kicked up a great deal of teasing that I wasn't used to. And don't get me wrong, I loved teasing my brothers. They bantered back and forth with me constantly until we were either laughing or wrestling on the ground, trying to work shit out.

But, this kind of teasing was laced with actual questions I didn't want to answer.

"Oh, come on, ya ladies' man. When you gonna find yourself a nice woman to settle down with?"

"You run around this town like a bat outta hell, and if you bang anymore of these innocent young gals you're gonna be up shit creek without a paddle when you want to turn around and have a family."

"Here comes Boone! And, of course, no girl on his arm. Why no girl, man? Those numbers in that little black book running a bit slim there?"

It wasn't that I disliked the jokes; I simply didn't like the insinuations that came with them. Just because everyone else in my family had settled down and popped out kids didn't mean that had to be my path. I didn't see children in my future. I didn't see myself staying with one woman for the rest of my life, either.

What are you doing?

The voice of my best friend echoed off the corners of my

mind, and I slid my hands down my sweating face. I groaned before I stepped back up to the bar of weights, dipping down to grip it with my trembling hands. I needed to exercise until I drowned out the voices. I needed to keep going until my brain decided to shut up.

Maybe then, I could get a decent night's sleep.

Seriously, man. What are you doing?

"One," I grunted as I hoisted the weights over my head.

You know she's out there, just like Sadie.

"Two," I hissed as I dropped the bar and did it again.

Why are you doing this to yourself?

"Three," I choked out as I thrust my hips, jolting the weights above my head once more.

But, I felt my arms giving way, so I dropped the weights to the mat.

"Fucking clean-and-jerks," I said breathlessly.

I pressed the heels of my hands into my eyes and tried to push the voices to the side. And if it were my brain trying to snap me out of things, I might have been able to. But, I'd never be able to bury DeShawn's voice.

"Fuck," I whispered.

I reached out for the floor and sat beside the weights I had dropped. I tilted my head back before I sprawled out on the mat, stretching my limbs and feeling my arms tingling with a need for rest. I lazily looked at my watch and sighed because it was damn near time for me to get to work.

And I sure as hell wasn't up for work today.

Are you just gonna flirt with our wives, Boone? Or, you gonna bring someone with you to these family dinners?

Ryan's voice echoed off the corners of my mind, and I clenched my jaw. It was bad enough that I didn't feel as if I were fulfilling my promise to my buddies I had lost overseas. It wasn't enough that I was the chief information security officer of my family's petrol company, and it sure as hell wasn't enough that I had more money than even God knew what to do with. My medals from my time in the Marines didn't matter. The sheer number of times people had saluted me didn't matter. Hell, the number of trophies I'd won in body-building competitions on the side wasn't even enough to validate my success.

Not with my family, anyway.

And when they made comments like that, it made me feel like I was failing my guys. My men. My best friends.

The boys I wanted to live my life for since they were no longer here to live theirs.

"Hey, are you done with those?"

The harsh voice ripped me from my trance, and I focused my eyes upward. As I looked up from the floor, I found a beautiful woman standing over me with her strawberry-blond hair tied up into a tight bun right on top of her head. Her piercing green eyes told me she wasn't shitting around with her day, and the way she cocked her hip out while she stood told me she was more perturbed than anything else.

Still, her striking beauty pulled me up and raised me to my feet.

"Yeah, yeah. I'm done," I said.

She nodded. "Thanks. I'll clean them down. My client needs to learn the correct form for squats."

I blinked. "Your client?"

She thumbed over her shoulder. "The woman in the gray sweatpants and the face full of makeup."

I looked over to where she had pointed, and I saw the young woman typing away on her phone. She had on a pair of tight gray sweatpants and a tank top that plunged much too deeply for someone just going to the gym first thing in the morning. Her hair was impeccably groomed, and for some reason, she deemed red lipstick and fake eyelashes necessary for a nice sweat-out in the musty weight room of the gym I had frequented since getting out of the Marines.

But, a sharp whistle pierced my eardrum, and I cupped my hand over my ear.

"What the fuck?" I asked.

The strawberry-blond woman pointed up at me. "No staring. That's the exact thing that makes women so uncomfortable. It's why they never come to the gym. Keep your eyes to yourself."

I playfully winked at her. "Sure about that?"

She ignored my question. "Now, if you don't mind, I need to get back to work. Heather!"

The girl on her phone didn't even look up from the screen. "Yep?"

"Let's get you in squat form. We'll just practice with the bar for now."

The girl nodded mindlessly. "Sure, yeah. Coming."

My eyes slid down the body of Mrs. Green Eyes, and I could've sworn she looked familiar. She must've just had that kind of face, though, because I couldn't pinpoint her.

"Well, I'll get out of your way. Just need to get my water bottle," I said.

The woman reached down and tossed it to me. "Here."

I caught it. "Thanks."

"Don't say I never did nothing for you," she murmured.

I wanted to ask her what the hell that meant, but I decided to leave it be. I only had twenty minutes to shower and get to work, and the last thing I needed to be was late. For work. Again.

Bryce will have my ass if I'm not in my office by nine.

"Well, nice meeting you," I said.

She waved her hand in the air as if to shoo me away. "Likewise. Heather!"

"What?" the girl asked flatly.

The woman snapped her fingers and pointed to the mat. "Either get over here now or leave. And since I know your father isn't going to be happy if you leave, you might as well come on and try to at least make the best of this."

I grinned. "Get her."

The woman glared at me. "You can go now."

I held up my hands in mock surrender. "All right, all right. I'm going."

I backed toward the door, though, and kept my eyes on the fiery strawberry-blonde with the hardened green eyes.

Dammit, she looked and felt so fucking familiar that I almost wondered if I were losing my memory or having some sort of prophetical dreams. My eyes explored her body as I tried to place her, but instead, I got lost in the slope of her curves. It was very clear to me that she was an employee of the gym and not simply because she was Heather's trainer.

Oh, no. The slope of her curves was trimmed and tailored. Obviously, she treated her body as the impeccable temple it deserved to be regarded as.

And dammit, it was a good thing I had to leave. Because when she started squatting down to demonstrate shit to her client, I felt my pelvis churning with need.

With wobbling legs and burning arms, I rushed off to the men's locker room and took the quickest shower of my life. I dried off and threw on my work clothes before stuffing my soaked gym clothes into my bag. With my wallet in my back pocket and the keys to my truck in my hand, I strutted my shit out of the locker room and headed for the smoothie stand.

I needed a double-dose of energy to get through my day.

"What can I getcha?" the cheery girl asked.

I gave her a kind smile. "A banana and matcha smoothie with two scoops of protein and two servings of B-vitamins."

She rang me up. "Anything else? An apple? A muffin? We have hardboiled eggs now, too."

I leaned forward. "Actually, I was hoping you could help me with something."

"I can do my best, sir."

I peeked over my shoulder toward the gym door and saw my beautiful fireball storming out the door. She charted a path down the hallway, keeping her eyes forward and her fists clenched at her sides. She looked pissed—very, very pissed. Pissed enough to throw those fists through a wall if we were surrounded by something other than plaster and cement.

"Must be rough with Heather," the girl murmured.

My eyes turned back to the smoothie woman. "So, you know of this, Heather."

She scoffed. "Who doesn't? She and her family are new in town, and she's about as spoiled as they come. Get this: she turned eighteen a couple of months ago, and her parents bought her a Ferrari. Brand new. Custom-made. Tinted windows. The works."

My eyebrows rose. "Anyone know much about this family?" Because I sure as hell had never heard of her, and it was rare for my family not to know about the inner workings of the small town we practically owned.

"Not much. Like I said, they're pretty new. They only moved into town a couple of weeks ago," the smoothie woman said.

I blinked. "How do you know what kind of car she got for her eighteen birthday, then?"

She giggled. "Rumors about people like that travel quickly around here. Shouldn't you already know that?"

I grinned. "I'd love to take a muffin. You got cream cheese?"

"Always, Mr. Boone."

I pulled my wallet out of my back pocket. "And while we're on the topic, who's the strawberry blonde who just stormed down the hallway? I saw her fussing around in there with that Heather girl. That her trainer or something?"

The girl took the cash I handed her. "That's Kate. She's one of our most loyal staff. She's worked here for a little while now, and she's one of the few full-time employees here."

Her name slapped me across the face. "Kate?"

"Mhm."

"As in, Kate Riley?"

The woman behind the counter handed back my change. "That's the one! Why? You know her or something?"

I tucked the change away in my pocket. "Or something, yeah."

Kate Riley was the girl I'd had a crush on back in high school. Kate Riley was the girl who had rejected me multiple times when I had attempted to ask her out. Kate Riley was the one woman on my track record I couldn't nail down, no matter how many times I had tried.

Kate Riley was the first girl who had ever caught my eye.

And maybe, just maybe, this was the universe giving me a chance to show that woman exactly what she had missed out on.

2

Kate

"And over here is our snack stand. Though, most of us call it 'Smoothie Stop.'"

Heather popped her gum and nodded her head. "Yep."

I tried hard not to smack her phone out of her hand. "This is where you'll come to get your after-workout protein shake. Now, this is probably one of the most important steps in your workout. Since you want to tone up and not lose weight, it's imperative to give your body something to create that muscle with right after you've put in all the work. So, you either want to order something with an extra scoop of protein, or something with peanut butter added if the drink already has protein in it."

She popped her gum again. "Got it."

"What can I getcha, Kate?" the woman behind the counter asked.

I puffed out my cheeks with a sigh. "Let me get an extra-large banana mocha smoothie with extra protein, and get my client a peanut butter, chocolate smoothie with the same. It'll be on me, Heather." I peeked over my shoulder and watched her wave her hand in the air.

"Just put it on my tab."

My voice fell flat. "This isn't a bar. You pay when you order something."

She rolled her eyes. "Fine, let me dig out my card."

"I said, I'm paying for your first one. So you don't lose anything if you don't like it."

The girl kept typing away on her phone as she nodded mindlessly, and dammit, I'd had enough of her air-headed attitude. I gathered up our smoothies and shoved one into her hand before essentially leading her out the front door myself. I waved goodbye as she stormed off to her car, angry at whatever the fuck a rich, spoiled brat had to be angry about.

And as I sipped my smoothy gruffly through my straw, I felt Marjorie—my boss—come up behind me.

"Went that well, huh?" she asked.

I rolled my eyes. "Oh, yeah. Peachy."

"Am I going to be getting an angry phone call from her father?"

I shrugged. "Probably."

She snickered. "I'll make sure to brace for it."

I sighed and made my way back to the lobby, where I wrapped around behind the desk. I sat off in a corner where Marjorie let me hang out on my lunch breaks while I chugged my smoothies right before my lunch-hour class. Salsa, of all things, was on the docket for this month. And I knew I could expect a great deal of working and stay-at-home mothers in the class who wanted to "spice up their lives" by learning dance moves they'd never be able to get their husbands to perform.

One of the many reasons why I preferred staying single.

However, once I got to my class to set up, I noticed a very familiar face in the crowd.

Mainly because he was the only man in the class.

I watched him carefully as he set up his station. He glanced at the other women, who kept whispering and blushing in his direction. Every once in a while, he offered their dry crotches a soft wink to get them giggling and blushing even more. I rolled my eyes at the show. Of course, Boone Remington would be in my class. Of course, he'd try to come after me again. He couldn't have me in high school, so it was round two for the brutish idiot.

I mean, the man was practically a gym rat back in the day —all muscles, no intelligence, and had used his body more than his mouth to get what he wanted. Girls threw themselves at his feet every time he flexed and smiled, but the posturing always made me shake my head.

He came from such a reputable family. And yet, he had turned out like that.

"All right, class!" I exclaimed as I clapped my hands. "Let's get this party started. Who's ready?"

The girls whooped and hollered as Boone grinned at me from his place in the middle of the dance floor, right in the midst of the throng of sexually starved wives and mothers.

With his focus clearly on me.

"Then, let's get to dancing!" I yelled.

I turned on the music and got my high knees going as I jogged my arms at my sides. Everyone followed my motions, including Boone, and I figured if I had to tolerate him for the next hour, the least I could do was make it worth my while. I mean, the flyer did say it was an intermediate class, and what was the point of an intermediate class if I didn't get straight into the more difficult moves?

It might be fun to watch him struggle at something for once.

"All right, everyone! Remember our basic moves from intro?"

The women nodded and gave me multiple thumbs-ups while Boone had his head on a swivel. He already looked as if he were beginning to panic, and it brought me all the joy in the world.

"Well, let's take it up a notch, shall we?" I called out.

The girls clapped their hands over their heads, and I started with some more intricate steps. Cross-overs and moving along the floor in a circle to the beat of the music. I wanted to teach them how to travel around the dance floor during our class. I wanted to show them that salsa wasn't stationary, but it could be morphed and folded into whatever they wanted it to be.

And all the while, I felt Boone's eyes on me.

It wasn't the first time a man had joined my class simply to ogle me. And every time, I always made sure to embarrass them without showing my intent. Usually, the guys never came back after I didn't pay them "special attention." But, sometimes, a few of the rare jerks needed a few classes of pure ass-kicking before they ducked back into the gym with their weights and their grunts and their protein drinks.

But, to my shock, Boone kept up.

Not only did he keep up, but he also actually started grabbing the other women and twirling them, dancing around the room as if we were in some sort of evening salsa club. The girls laughed and clapped as he went in a circle, offering his hand and bowing his head before turning them into him. I felt myself going red in the face. This was my fucking class, and who the hell did he think he was trying to take over like that?

He had some sick moves, though.

Seems the brutish man with a clean-shaven face has some secrets after all.

Still, it didn't lessen my annoyance. Boone ran away with my class so badly that I couldn't keep up instruction because all the women wanted to do was dance with the handsome new recruit. I shook my head as I walked into the corner to dab my face. I clocked the time, letting the girls have their fun since they probably weren't getting any at home in the first place.

But, the second the clock hit ten to one, I whistled at the top of my lungs. "Class dismissed, everyone! Great job!" I exclaimed.

Everyone was sweatier than I'd ever seen them before, and somehow that pissed me off even more. Not only had Boone Remington swept into my classroom and stolen my thunder, but he had worked them to death, and not once did they complain or even consider letting up. I'd never seen these women work out so hard in all their lives. And it pissed me off that it took my high school nemesis to turn the class around.

"Kate Riley."

His smooth voice appeared behind me as the gaggle of women made their way out of the room. I peered at them through the wall-to-wall mirrors to my left and saw their eyes lingering on Boone's form, and I glared at their reflections. I kept glaring until they were gone, leaving only myself and the overgrown college kid standing in the corner.

"Hello, Boone," I said as I turned around. I drew in a silent breath and forced myself to stomach his presence.

"Nice class," he said with a grin.

I brushed past him, heading for my water bottle. "Maybe don't stare so much next time, though."

His chuckle resonated behind me. "Trust me, I wasn't the one staring nearly as much as you were."

I shook my head slowly. "You were cocky and brutish in high school, and it seems nothing has changed."

He slipped in front of me and leaned against the mirror. "Your words would hurt if they were true. But, I promise you they aren't."

"Could've fooled me."

"Why don't you let me take you out to dinner, then, and prove it?"

I barked with laughter as I slung my towel over my shoulder. "While your boldness is impressive, I'm going to have to pass."

He smiled. "Making the same mistakes twice, are we?"

"Trust me, Boone, turning you down was never a mistake."

I picked up my bag and slung it over my shoulder, heading straight for the door. I didn't care if he stayed in this room to rot; all I wanted was to be away from him. Yet, I felt his eyes staring into the back of my head, and it caused me to pause just shy of the closed door that led out into the hallway. "Spit it out," I said.

I heard his footsteps coming closer behind me. "What do I need to do in order to get a chance with you?"

I shrugged. "I'm sure a big boy like you can figure it out eventually."

I walked out into the hallway, leaving him in my dust, and I felt more triumphant than ever before. Though, I didn't like the way my pelvis felt. It felt... warm. Inviting. Maybe a bit too wet for the lack of sweating I'd just done in class. And while I tried not to pay attention to it, I couldn't fully ignore it.

Boone looked a lot different than he had in high school, and for the better, too.

And I hated how easy on the eyes he had become.

Because the man really needed a fucking change of personality to go along with it.

3

Boone

Ityped away at my computer as my eyes trailed along what most people would've considered nonsensical lines of gibberish. But, to me? They were scores of data waiting to be downloaded and pilfered through after a long weekend. Mondays were always my worst days. I had to filter through data that poured into our system all day and all night while the office was unmanned, and sometimes I'd have to stay until midnight or later just to get it all sorted. But I dealt with the most sensitive systems and information stores that my family's petrol company had in their grasp.

So, I took my job that seriously.

"Wyatt!" Bella squealed.

"And you thought I wouldn't find you," he said with a chuckle.

"Wyatt, stop! That tickles!"

I heard a soft thud against my office wall before Bella moaned. I rolled my eyes at the sounds of their kissing wafting beneath the crack of the door. I shook my head and reached for my headphones, placing them over my head before I got back to work. After turning up the music to drown out their public displays of workplace affection, my mind started churning.

I was incredibly happy my brothers had found love and shit like that, but I knew I wasn't cut out for that life. I'd lost way too many people I cared about, and I worked far too many hours to give someone like a dedicated woman the attention she deserved. All of my brothers worked odd hours now in order to placate their wives and girlfriends and families. I was the only one keeping a standard business shift. I was the only one who didn't gripe about overtime any longer. And when the shit hit the fan with their families, guess who they called to pick up the slack at work?

Me, that's who.

So, who the hell would they call if I got wrapped up in a lady friend, too?

Boone.

My hands froze, and I squeezed my eyes shut as the smell of sand wafted up my nose.

"No, no, no," I murmured.

Boone, please.

I ripped my headphones off my head. "Not now. Not right now. I'm in the middle of—"

I looked down and saw Michael in my arms, bleeding from the side of his neck. I wrapped my hand against it, placing as much pressure on it as I could while trying not to choke off his air supply.

"Just keep breathing; help will be here soon," I said.

But, when Michael coughed, it tainted his lips red. "Rem, listen to me."

I shook my head. "Dammit, Sanchez. Shut up and keep your strength."

I gazed around at the scattered bodies all around us. I curled up behind the overturned Humvee as I pulled Michael into my arms. I held him close and squeezed my eyes shut. I pressed my hand deeper against his neck.

"Pro—promise me some—something," Michael choked out.

I swallowed back my tears. "No promises. You're not giving up on me."

"Rem."

His voice sounded so weak, and it broke my heart. "Yeah?"

"Look at me."

I forced my eyes to peel themselves open, and I looked down into the light of his irises. A light that was dwindling with every bullet that ricocheted against our Humvee that had been blown to bits.

"What?" I asked.

Rem coughed, splattering blood against my face. "Promise me you'll be happy. That you'll—live a good life. One that you'll—be proud of."

And as my lip started quivering, I nodded my head. "You have my word."

I ripped my headphones off and stood from my chair. I stood up with such a force that it rolled back and hit the opposing wall, causing Bella to yelp again. I wiped at the tears threatening to rush down my face as silence blanketed the hallway just beyond my door.

But then, a terrifying sound hit my ears.

The sound of an alarm going off on my computer.

"What the—"

I saw the television screen to my far left blinking red, and I scrambled to find my chair.

"No, no, no, no," I murmured, "this can't be happening."

A knock came at my door before Wyatt's voice sounded. "Boone?"

I sat down and started typing away. "Come in or leave me alone."

My door swung open. "Is that what I think it is?"

Then, the television screen right in front of me started blinking and going off with an alarm, too.

"What the fuck?" I hissed.

I heard Wyatt murmur something to Bella before he slipped into my office and closed the door.

"What do you need?" he asked.

I scoffed. "You and Bella not to have sex against the walls of my office."

He hunched over my desk, his face next to mine. "Noted. But, also, what the hell is this?"

My fingers typed as quickly as they could. "I'm not sure

yet, but it looks like we're being hacked."

He nodded slowly. "I thought you said that couldn't happen since you created the systems yourself."

I snickered. "Yeah, well, first time for everything, I suppose. Go tell the guys. We might have to pull the plug on some things if I can't back-trace this bullshit."

I moved as quickly as I could, but one by one, my screens started to light up. We were definitely being hacked, and every time I tried to trace what the fuck was going on, I hit a wall. I'd never seen anything like it. Not in the Marines, not when deployed, and certainly not on any server or with any interface having to do with our company.

And I started growing worried.

"All right, is everything looking good in here?" Wyatt asked.

I motioned to my blinking red screens. "Does it look okay in here, man?"

"Is there anything I can do to help?"

I slammed my hands onto the keyboard and stood up. "Unplug. We have to unplug now. They've breached the second to last firewall."

I reached behind all of my computers and started yanking out the plugs as Wyatt barked orders down the hallway. I heard footsteps scurrying about, trying to get to their systems as quickly as possible. I sat back down and pulled out my laptop, remotely deactivating the bulk of our systems while my computers and televisions powered down.

But, I still had no idea who the hell was attacking our

systems.

"Yes, all of it," Wyatt said harshly, "unplug all of it. Now. Yes, even that. Just do it already!"

I started typing away on my keyboard. "Come on, you son of a bitch. Let's see what you've got."

I pulled up the local interface on my laptop and tried to lock this person out of the system. The good news was that whoever was attempting this, they tried it with a virus first. That meant they still didn't have access to our closed-circuit systems and needed a way to drill in before being able to do anything. And that meant I could at least trace it to the computer it had first appeared on. The virus itself wasn't the issue, though. It was what the virus had implanted.

"Holy fuck," I murmured.

I started putting up miniature guards in an attempt to lure the hacker away from our most sensitive systems. But, every time I attempted to draw them in another direction, they bypassed me. It was almost like they knew what they were looking for... as if they were familiar with a system like this.

But, for the life of me, I knew we didn't employ anyone with anywhere near this kind of capability.

"Status update?" Wyatt asked.

"Everything unplugged?" I asked.

"I just unplugged the last of our routers and shut things off at the circuit breaker. It was the quickest way to get things done. Everyone downstairs is working on unplugging every-thing, though."

I nodded slowly. "Good. Make sure no one deletes

anything. I know how the hacker got into our system."

"How?"

I held up my finger before I went back to typing. "Whoever this is, they're good. They've got knowledge of what they're looking for, too. They're not just blindly downloading shit."

Wyatt raced to perch beside me. "You mean someone from the inside is doing this?"

I shook my head. "No. They had to implant a virus into our network before they could drill in. Probably a piece of spam mail that got opened."

"Fucking hell, I know who that could be, too," he murmured.

"It's going to take me on into the night to figure out who the fuck this is, though. Their IP signal is bouncing everywhere, and it's going to take a serious moment with my equipment to get it nailed down."

"What can we do to facilitate?"

I peeked up at him. "No plugging anything back in until I give the word. I'll operate from my laptop, as should you guys, but only from remote internet sources. No using our internet until I can make sure it's scrubbed clean and nailed down tight."

"Remote hotspots and laptops. Got it. Anything else?"

I sighed. "Leave me alone so I can get this done."

He patted my shoulder. "I can do that, too. I'll send everyone home for the day."

I held my finger up. "If you're going to do that, get some

statements. I want to know what everyone in this building was doing when this first happened. We'll back up their statements with security cameras footage."

"Done and done. See you soon."

Then, I was alone with my thoughts once again.

It took me damn near thirty minutes to corner the hacker, but I managed to do it. I had backed them into a corner before starting up my rooting program that not only refused to let their signal go but dug into the bouncing around to rake through their data in order to provide an IP address. It... wasn't exactly legal. Especially since I kind of usurped the general code from the Marine installments where I had been stationed during my career.

But, the way I saw it, imitation was the highest form of flattery.

And who the hell else was going to be smart enough to call me out on it?

Except for maybe this person.

After cornering the little fuck, I locked them out for good and scrubbed the system. Thank fuck, we backed up all of our shit onto massive servers; otherwise, we'd be back at square one. I knew it would be a long night rebuilding these firewalls and security protocols I had put in place after being given this job straight out of the military. But, if someone had found a hole to exploit—even in the form of an email virus—that gave me tools and information to work with to build a more secure system.

Even if it took me all fucking week to get it done.

❧ 4 ❧

Kate

A couple of days passed, and not once did I see Boone resurface at the gym. He wasn't in any of my classes, he wasn't peacocking in any of the hallways, and I sure as hell didn't see him at the weight racks. Good riddance, if anyone asked me about it because my gym didn't need that kind of energy in it in the first place.

Stupid little fuckboys.

There was a time in my life where I would have found the presence of a man like him attractive. There was a time in my life where the sight of Boone Remington would've sent sparks flying between my bosoms. But, that time was long gone. I wasn't a giddy little college girl ready to sink herself into alcohol and dick just to get by without feeling. That wasn't who I was any longer.

And any reminder of who I used to be made me sad more than anything else.

"Kate!"

I turned at the sound of my name and saw Marjorie power-walking down the hallway at me.

"Kate, Kate, Kate, Kate. I'm so glad I caught you," she said as she approached me.

I smiled. "Do I need to pick up another class tonight?"

She shook her head as she panted for breath. "No, no. Nothing like that. You actually have a last-minute lunch hour session today. I've found someone to take over your salsa class."

I blinked. "Wait, why? I'd get paid more money to—"

She shook her head. "Not with this person. They're apparently paying four times your hourly rate just to book that one hour with you."

Fucking hell. "It's Boone, isn't it?"

She eyed me sternly. "Is that an issue?"

I shook my head. "No, ma'am. Not one bit. I'll go right now and get prepared for the lesson."

She nodded. "Good. Because we certainly wouldn't want to anger yet another donator to our gym, right?"

I sighed. "So, you heard from Heather's father?"

"I didn't just hear from him; he almost pulled his entire funding schedule from us. I don't know what you did to his daughter, but she was crying when she got home."

I furrowed my brow. "Crying?"

"Yep."

"I didn't do anything except—"

But, Marjorie held up her hand. "Trust me, I know. I told him I'd look back at the security footage to figure out what happened, and I did. I made sure to call him back and let him know that there were no signs of impropriety on our end, but that his daughter was breaking a fair number of rules that you're obligated to comment on unless she wants her lessons contract broken."

"And how did he take that?"

She shrugged. "About as well as can be expected. But, he had no grounds to stand on, and I stand by the integrity of this gym. However, that means we need to be very careful for a little while. And that means you're taking this lesson with the Remington boy, and you're going to put on a smile while you do it. Understood?"

"One hundred percent."

She patted my shoulder. "Great. Now, go, get ready. Your lesson starts in ten minutes."

While part of me wanted to spit in his general direction, when Boone walked through the weight room doors for his session, I tried to put on my best professional face. I didn't have to hold it long, though, because he didn't look too pleased to be there, either.

"You okay?" I asked as he approached me.

He walked around me and headed for the weight racks. I furrowed my brow and jogged after him, wondering what the fuck he was about to do. I watched as he picked up some barbells and held them at his side, eyeing my reflection hotly in the mirror as our eyes met.

But he didn't answer me.

"Boone, what are you doing? We have a lesson, so we should probably start—"

He whipped around, swinging the barbells at his side. "Kate, you and I both know that I don't need a trainer. But, I do need a workout partner. Someone who can keep me accountable and stop me from going too far and hurting my body in the process."

I clicked my tongue. "All right."

"So, pick up some barbells, and let's get to work."

I quirked an eyebrow. "You're pompous, but you're also correct. Just watching you in here a few days ago showed me you don't need anyone to help you out in this arena. But, you didn't have to pay for my time to have a workout partner."

He lifted the barbells over his head. "I did if I wanted *you* as my workout partner. And thanks for admitting that you were staring the other day. I thought I was being watched."

His words infuriated me, and if steam coming out of my ears were possible, it would have happened. Still, he was paying me a hell of a lot of money just to work out with him, and I hadn't yet had my daily workout.

Let's see what the big boy's got, then.

I went over and picked up a moderately weighted set of barbells and hung them at my sides. I brought my arms up to a ninety-degree angle before pushing them over my head, then slowly—and with control—brought them back down to my sides. I watched Boone in the mirror as he pumped out reps at a blinding pace, almost as if he were doing high-interval-intensity-training bursts before taking a thirty-second rest.

Except, the man didn't rest.

"Boone, take a breather."

"Boone, go down ten pounds, so you don't hurt yourself."

"Your feet need to be a little bit more apart. You ruin your knee joints that way."

"Yeah, don't stretch like that, do it like this. It'll get more of your lower back in the mix."

"For God's sake, go down ten pounds."

He wiped the sweat from his brow after dropping his rack of weights. "Do you talk to all of your clients that way?"

I shrugged. "Just the stubborn ones.

I nudged him out of the way and positioned myself for a set of clean-and-jerks. I saw Boone's smirk in the mirror as he tucked his hands beneath his armpits, crossing his arms over his chest. I bent down in perfect form and gripped the bar, readying myself for a max-out rep. But dammit, I threw up five maxed out clean-and-jerks before I set the bar down as easily as I had lifted it.

"Wow. I'm impressed," Boone said.

I panted for air. "Try not to slam the bar down next time. That can crack the floor beneath all of this padding, and that takes a lot of money to fix so it won't cause foundational issues."

He walked back up to the bar as I stepped off to the side.

"You know a lot about this place. How long have you been working here?"

I shrugged as I dabbed at the sweat on my brow. "A little while now. I don't really keep track."

The truth of the matter was that I didn't want to talk about it. My life hadn't turned out at all like I had thought it would, and the less I focused on it, the better. My life had taken drastic turns, and I had ridden with them as best as I possibly could while also trying not to focus on how alone I felt most of the time.

Around and around and around we went, traveling slowly across the gym as we touched on a little bit of everything. The determined look behind Boone's eyes told me that he wasn't trying to work on anything in particular, and I knew that mindset all too well. That was the mindset that came with a need to forget. A need to push things out of the way and do something repetitive that required no thought.

I wondered what weighed so heavily on his mind.

Why do you care? He's just some stuck-up jock who never grew up.

Still, the workout was one of the best I'd ever had, and when our time came to a close, I was almost reluctant to let him go. I felt reinvigorated and ready for a good meal. I felt like I was on top of the world. And as I watched Boone chug his water, my eyes followed a droplet across his jawline that didn't quite make it between his lips.

It wasn't until his water bottle started crackling that I stopped staring.

"Well, I'll see you tomorrow," he said. He crushed the remaining part of the bottle in his hand and tossed it into a trash can.

"Sure thing. I'll be here," I said.

Boone chuckled. "No, I mean, I've booked out your lunch hour for our workouts through the month. So, I actually will see you tomorrow."

My eyebrows slowly raised. "That's a hell of a lot of money for training you don't need."

He shrugged. "I'm not doing anything else with it."

"Then, I guess I'll see you tomorrow."

I watched as Boone picked up his things and made his way out of the gym. And as the door closed behind him, I heaved a heavy sigh. I hated to admit it, but I was actually looking forward to our session tomorrow. I was essentially getting paid to release stress in my second most favorite fashion, and I was getting paid much, much more than usual to do it.

Don't let him get under your skin. He made your life a living nightmare.

I drew in a sharp breath of air and turned back around. But, I didn't really focus on one particular thing. My mind swam with so many thoughts, and most of them were about Boone. That man was once the boy who had made my life so miserable after I had turned him down that I had begged my foster parents to homeschool me. I begged them to pull me out and let me finish high school by taking the GED in order to test out altogether. I had turned him down twice, and he had decided to follow me around and mock me. Call me names. Spray glitter at me as I walked down the hallway and stuff my locker with things like rotten fruit and shaving cream.

He tormented me after I wouldn't go on a date with him, and the last thing I needed to be doing was empathizing with him. So, I held my head high and decided not to give him the satisfaction of warming to him, pitying him, or taking the time to try to figure him out, even if he weren't here to bear witness to the fact that I couldn't care less about what bothered him.

Boone

Bryce balked. "Mr. Blanchard?"

Wyatt scoffed. "You can't be serious."

Will ripped the documents out of my hand. "Let me see those."

I shrugged. "You can pore over them all you want, but my system doesn't lie."

Ryan narrowed his eyes. "So, you're telling us that after almost forty-eight hours of combing through whatever it was that happened Monday afternoon, that the IP address you found that hacked our network back-traced to someone on our board of investors?"

I nodded. "Looks like it."

Will slapped the documents against Bart's chest. "I can't fucking believe it."

I snickered. "Neither can I. I'm pretty sure we're all in agreement that he doesn't have the technological know-how to do something like this, either."

Bryce shook his head. "Mr. I Don't Know Why My Phone Won't Turn On? Hell, no. Not in a million years."

Bart handed me the papers after he was done looking at them. "And you're sure there's been no mistake?"

I shook my head as I rolled the papers up and stuck them into my back pocket. "If I could be anything more than one hundred percent sure, that's what I'd be. This is his IP address."

Bryce clicked his tongue. "So, someone used Mr. Blanchard's computer to hack us?"

Will sighed. "Which begs the question as to who has access to his computer."

I cracked my neck. "I'm still looking into things, but here's what I know. This computer isn't only registered to Mr. Blanchard, but it's registered to his house. This isn't a work computer of his. It's a personal one."

"Jesus," Bart whispered.

"So, that means whoever did this has intimate access to Mr. Blanchard's things," Ryan said.

"Hold on," Wyatt said.

I watched as he rushed into his office, and I furrowed my brow. "Wyatt?"

"I said, hold on! Give me a second!"

I peeked back at my brothers. "Any idea at all?"

But, they simply shrugged or shook their heads.

"Got it," Wyatt hissed.

"Got what?" I called out.

He charged back into the hallway with a stapled pack of papers in his hand. "Take a look at this." He handed them to me, and I started flipping through them before I realized what it was.

"Why am I looking at Mr. Blanchard's resume?"

Wyatt slapped the papers with the back of his hand. "Would you just read, asshole?"

I glared at him. "You get one pass with me, all right?"

Bryce pinched the bridge of his nose. "Simmer down and read it, please? We've got more pressing matters at hand."

I cleared my throat and started scouring his resume, but it didn't take me long to see it. Apparently, Mr. Blanchard had worked as the head of a cybersecurity department long before he came into his father's wealth. The Blanchard's were known for their financial services, beginning with a business Blanchard, Sr. had started when the man was fresh out of college. The small bank Senior had started grew into a multi-billion-dollar corporation, and when he passed, he left everything to the man currently sitting on our board of investors.

But before that, he was the CISO of his father's financial empire.

I scoffed. "You mean to tell me a man who struggles with his fucking cell phone once held the title of CISO? I don't believe it for a second."

"Let me see that," Bryce said as he ripped it out of my hand.

Wyatt was so upset that he was red in the face. "And you guys know me. You know I vetted shit very, very well with those investors. So, if he's sitting on that board, it means my vetting checked out."

Bart pointed at Wyatt. "He's got a point. Wyatt is nothing, if not thorough."

Wyatt nodded. "Thank you."

I dug the heels of my hands into my eyes. "Okay, so at least in theory, he's got some skills underneath his belt. But why would he want to hack us? What's his motive?"

Bryce cleared his throat. "I mean, if he knows anything about this world, he had to know Boone would find him."

I snapped my fingers. "Exactly. That doesn't make any sense, either. So, what gives?"

Wyatt shrugged. "I mean, I can give the man a call and tell him what we found. Maybe it's just a simple case of someone using his shit to do some nefarious, well, other shit."

Will shook his head, though. "No, we have to come at this with a cool head; otherwise, he'll just clam up. And right now? I don't like the color of your face."

Bart chuckled. "He's also got a point there. But, if any of this is the case and Mr. Blanchard really has no idea what the hell is up, then that means someone who wants information we have has access to his stuff."

I nodded. "*Intimate* access."

We went back and forth for a while, talking through all of

the evidence we had at our disposal and trying to figure out how to proceed. It was a sensitive subject no matter how things got sliced, though. By the time we were done talking the damn issue to death, the solution in front of our eyes was pretty simple: wait until it happened again and see if it back-traced to the same IP address.

"I really don't like this," I murmured.

Ryan put his hand on my shoulder. "But, if there's anyone who's prepared for something like this, it's you."

Will eyed me carefully. "Our security protocols are back up and running, right?"

I nodded. "Right."

"Any way you can tone them back down to what they were before?"

I blinked. "You willingly want me to downgrade our security systems back to the original form after I spent damn near all fucking week trying to beef them up?"

Wyatt wiggled his finger at me. "Actually, that makes sense."

I groaned. "Will someone fill me in, please?"

Bart chuckled. "What they want to do is give the idea that we've come to the conclusion that nothing was a threat. If we restore the security systems back to their regular mode—or whatever it is you call it—it'll look like we dug into everything, and nothing nefarious was found. Especially since they didn't get their hands on anything, right?"

I shrugged. "I mean, not that I know of, but I'm not done going through everything yet."

Wyatt patted my back. "Then, get to it. Downgrade the systems, let's see what happens, and when the person strikes again—and they will if they don't have what they want—we'll be there to either catch them, or we'll have enough evidence to take to Mr. Blanchard before we start asking some hard questions."

I nodded but reluctantly. "All right, if you guys think it'll work. But, all I'm saying is that at no point in time during my military experience did we ever intentionally downgrade security protocols to lure someone in. That shit gets dangerous quickly."

Bryce smiled. "Then, it's a good thing you're working with us."

Wyatt stepped into the middle of the circle. "And speaking of working with us, Will and Bryce..."

Bart groaned. "Not now, Wyatt."

But, all he did was hold up his hand. "Bryce, Will. Have you guys given any thought to buying out the company from the board of investors? It might prevent stuff like this from ever occurring again."

Bryce snickered. "One step at a time, man. But, if we're really going to hash this out, then the answer is 'yes.' I'm on board."

Wyatt grinned with delight as his eyes moved over to Will. "And for you? Did you speak with Sadie like you mentioned you would?

However, Will only smiled back. "Nice placement. You're

a hell of a salesman. I applaud your efforts. But, no. We still don't have an answer for you."

Wyatt clasped his hands behind his back. "One down, one to go."

I chuckled and shook my head. "Try not to yell too loudly in your office when you get back inside."

The guys fell apart, laughing at that statement, and it caused Wyatt to pull away from all of us. I knew he was pissed that Will still wasn't ready with an answer, but something like this took time to put together. The only reason I had given my answer so quickly was that I didn't have anyone to consult. I thought it was a great idea, so I went for it.

None of my other brothers had that luxury, though.

Still, I wondered in the back of my mind if our board of investors had caught wind of what we were planning to do. We had made those men a great deal of money throughout their tenure on the board, and money was always a great motive to pull shit like this.

Maybe Mr. Blanchard is behind this, after all.

If there were a chance that he even suspected what we were up to, that might provide an answer to what the hacker was searching for. Maybe they were trying to locate information about buying them out, which they wouldn't find because that kind of sensitive information was kept on an off-site server that wasn't hooked up to our regular network.

The upside to that was they'd never find what they were looking for.

The downside was that we could expect multiple attacks before they figured that out.

Is it really possible, though?

I mean, the only way for Mr. Blanchard to have caught wind about this would have been to eavesdrop on one of our conversations. Either that, or he'd have to hack our personal emails in the process. While the second suggestion seemed more plausible, I would've known if our emails had been hacked. And there was no evidence that something of the sort had occurred.

"Earth to Boone, you okay?" Bryce asked.

His voice snapped me out of my thoughts. "Just running some scenarios through my mind."

"Want someone to bounce them off of?"

I shook my head. "Maybe when I've got more than just theories. But, there's no need to panic anyone over basic thoughts."

He patted my shoulder. "Well, if you need anyone, let me know. Okay?"

I nodded. "You know I always do."

But, there was something in his eyes that hinted at something more. Something behind his gaze gave me the impression that he wasn't simply talking about the information we had just tossed around.

"We're always here. Never forget that," Bryce said.

I sighed. "I know, man. I know."

He smiled softly. "Good. See you at family dinner on Sunday?"

I chuckled. "You know damn good and well, I don't miss a home-cooked meal."

He started walking backward down the hallway. "Don't we know it!"

I waved him off before I slipped into my office, readying myself for another long night. I had my work cut out for me if I were going to find the signature trail the hacker had left behind. And when someone hacked a system like mine, there was always a trail to be had. Even if they didn't mean to leave one, there was still a method in the madness.

I only hoped I could uncover it before something worse happened.

6

Kate

I looked at my watch before gazing at the gym door and tapping my foot. Boone was late. Ten minutes late, to be exact. He hadn't called to cancel, he hadn't called to say he needed to postpone, and he sure as hell hadn't called to tell anyone he'd be running late. So, there I was, standing in the middle of the weight room, looking like a damn idiot. Until finally, he came charging through the door.

I sighed. "Great. Finally. All right, how do you feel about—"

He soared past me. "It's cardio day. I'm hitting the treadmill first."

I paused. "Well, then. Okay."

I followed him over to the treadmills, where I kept up his

pace during a brief warm-up. Then, we hopped off and started doing jumping lunges. I tapped my knees against my elbows for a set of ten before taking a five-second break. Then, I did five of those in a row beside Boone before heading over to the weights. We utilized light weights—at least five pounds beneath our minimum—and did speed lunges across the length of the weight room.

And during all of this, Boone didn't say a word.

Still, I kept up his pace, despite the fact that his pace almost kicked my ass. I sure as hell wasn't going to let this man beat me in anything, though, so I kept clocking him from time to time with my eyes to get my bearings as to what he was doing and how quickly he was traveling back and forth across the floor.

Except, he kept picking up his pace.

Around and around we went, silently competing with one another until we were practically sprinting through our workout session.

Treadmill, jumping lunges, lightweight lunges, jumping jacks, pause.

Jumping jacks, lightweight lunges, jumping lunges, treadmill, pause.

Over and over again, back and forth through the routine. And all the while, I heaved for air as I made sure Boone didn't get the better of me. My body dripped with sweat, and my clothes clung to me. I felt my lungs heaving for air and knew I needed to slow down, but my pride wouldn't let me. Every time Boone upped his weights, so did I. Every time he added an extra workout to our circuit training, I added it two-fold.

He still kicked my ass, though.

Because when I had to stop and bend over to keep the room from spinning, he was still jogging away on the treadmill.

"Need some water?" he asked.

I flipped him off before I stood up straight and held my hands over my head.

"Looks like you need a razor, too," he chuckled.

"Fuck you," I spat.

I looked over at the clock on the wall and realized that it was five minutes until one. Our training session had been over ten minutes ago, and I couldn't move toward the door quickly enough. There was no need to start drama with Boone. No need to bite off his head. But, the sooner I got him out of my daily picture, the better off I'd be. I had things I needed to do with my time that didn't amount to dealing with his spoiled little attitude.

I didn't dismiss him, though. If he wanted to keep going until he broke something, that was on him. But, my paid time with him was up. I grabbed a towel as I stormed out of the gym, wiping myself off while I carved a path toward the showers. I slammed my hip against the door and barged my way in as a gaggle of girls was coming out. They didn't look much older than college freshmen, and a pang of hurt wafted through my system.

What a waste my life has been.

I knew what I needed. A nice, hot-ass shower. And with the locker room empty during the quietest times in this place, I'd be able to take my time. I grabbed the disinfectant we kept in bottles around the gym and sprayed down the last shower to the left. It was a bit darker than most, but also a smidge bigger, which gave me enough room to sit and rest my legs if I needed.

I drenched that shower in cleaning solution before I used the showerhead to spray everything down the drain. Then, I stripped my clothes off my sticky body and hopped in. Before someone slipped in behind me.

"What the—"

I squealed against the hand that clapped down against my mouth. My eyes widened as my fists started swinging, but the person who backed in behind me already had me pinned against the wall. My cheek pressed against the tile. The massive hand pressing against my mouth held my lips shut. And when I heard the shower curtain slide closed, I kicked my leg back.

But, the person behind me simply spread their legs, and I almost slipped and fell to the floor.

"Help! Someone help me!" My screams came out as nothing but murmurs, though. "*Help!*"

Then, a voice sounded against the shell of my ear. "Tell me you don't want this, too."

Boone's voice settled over my conscious mind, and my nipples automatically puckered. Boone was behind me? What the hell was going on? I tried to shuffle around to see him, but he kept me pinned to the tile with his strength.

And I felt the bulging of his cock against my ass crack as my body heated with need.

"Just tell me to leave, and I will. I'm going to take my hand down now, okay?"

I nodded, and I felt his hand fall away. But he still wouldn't let me turn around.

"Boone, what the hell are you doing?" I hissed.

"Just tell me 'no,' and I'm gone," he said.

I couldn't, though, and that was the kicker. I couldn't deny the fact that he felt amazing pressed against my body. I couldn't deny the fact that even his sweat smelled sweet. I couldn't even deny the fact that I felt relieved that it was him and not someone—anyone—else behind me in that shower.

But, I kept my wits about me. "So, you couldn't have me in high school, which means you're going to force yourself into my shower now? Is that it?"

His nose nuzzled the nape of my neck. "Like I said, a simple 'no' will suffice."

I scoffed. "I've already given you that three times in your life, and you still won't take the hint."

"I'm not asking you on a date this time, Kate."

And despite my rational mind telling me to call out for help, I simply sighed. "I hope you know this won't change how much I absolutely cannot stand you."

He chuckled. "Then, that makes two of us."

His hands fell to my hips, and he whipped me around before he pulled me against his body. My eyes gazed up into his and the carnal lust rushing around behind them made my nipples pucker even harder. His hand found the tendrils of my hair, and he pulled back my head, exposing my pulse point to the hot water.

And when I felt his tongue touch down against my skin, I shuddered. "Wow," I whispered.

His teeth quickly replaced his tongue, and my knees grew weak. But dammit, I wouldn't even let him have the best of me in this form, either. I gripped his soaked shirt and tilted my head back up, crashing our lips together in a heated kiss. And when his tongue wrapped around mine, it shot me into a completely different universe.

Boone's hands pawed at my skin. He quickly picked me up and pinned me against the tile wall. My fingers raked through his hair, gripping the short chunks to gain leverage. I bucked against him as he shimmied his wet shorts down, his cock exposed to the hot water. And as he kissed down the back of my throat, I raked my teeth along his lower lip before I bit down a little too hard.

"Fuck," he grunted.

I giggled. "Serves you right for being an arrogant asshole."

He ripped my hands away from his hair and pinned them above my head. Then, he took the smallest step back to survey his work. With my legs still wrapped around him, his eyes cased my body. And when they stopped at my puckered peaks, he licked his lips.

"Even your body betrays you, Katie."

Hearing that name was enough to give me the strength to rip my hands out of his grasp. His eyes widened as I gripped his shirt, pulling him closer back to me. I glared at him as my teeth gnashed together. Anger unlike anything I'd ever experienced surged through my veins.

And as he stared at me with curious eyes, I practically growled at him. "Don't you ever call me that again. Ever. You got it?"

He nodded. "Yeah, I got it, Kate."

I shoved him away, but he didn't so much as flinch. I panted for a little bit, trying to control my rage as I felt it ebbing back down into its darkened box in the corner of my soul. This man angered me more than I could stand. Hell, my entire life did that.

But, something was etching itself across his face that gave him a softer look. And I wondered what he was thinking.

In seconds, though, the look was gone, and the carnal man who had shoved himself into my shower was back.

And as our lips fell together once more, I rolled my hips against his thickened girth before his cock slid effortlessly into my depths.

7

Boone

I growled as I sank into her depths. Holy fucking hell, she was the tightest little thing I'd felt around my dick in a very long time. I drank down the taste of her tongue and let mine slide across the roof of her mouth, shivering her against my body. She was perfection in a bottle. Her toned curves gave me life, and her luscious tits sucked it right back out of me. And while part of me wanted to explore her gorgeous body properly, the stressed-out part of me simply wanted to get off.

And judging by the way her pussy pulsed around me, she needed the release as well.

"Fucking hell," I grunted.

"Shit," she hissed.

I pounded into her deeply as the sounds of my skin slapping against hers filled the space around her. I'd say between us, but there wasn't much space there once our pelvises fell together. I twisted my hips, stroking her swollen clit as it peeked out from between a delectable set of pussy lips that kept swallowing my cock.

And after kissing down Kate's neck, my eyes fell to our connection. "Holy God, you're so wet," I panted.

Her nails raked down my arms, and the sensation made my toes curl. I pressed my hands into the tiled wall, watching as my cock disappeared time and time again between her legs. Her juices streaked my dick, painting a unique picture across my canvas that mesmerized me with every stroke.

That was, until she fisted my hair and pulled my lips back to hers.

I moved my arms and hooked them beneath her legs before I folded them toward her body. Her mouth gasped and moaned with pleasure as her kisses fell away. The rest of my dick slid deeply inside of her body, causing her to cry out as I pressed her helplessly against the wall.

"Oh, shit. Boone. Holy fuck, don't stop."

Goddammit, I'd been waiting years for her to say my name like that.

I thrust against her and lost myself in her warmth. In her smell. In the way, her naked skin felt against my own. I regretted not taking off my shirt as she spread herself for me, that pussy of hers opening wide to devour my cock whole. Her bouncing tits caught my eyes, and I reached down with my teeth, capturing one of her nipples between them. Then, I sucked her peak into my mouth and groaned against her skin.

"Oh, fuck," she whimpered.

Her pussy started collapsing against my cock, and it caused my hips to shutter. I slid my hands up the backs of her legs until my fingers wrapped around her ankles. I raised up, watching her head fall back against the wall helplessly as I spread and maneuvered her legs around, tightening and opening that pussy for my cock's pleasure.

Then, her hands came crashing down against my shoulders before her nails curled into my skin.

"I'm coming. I'm coming. Boone—holy fu—I can't—you —shit!"

I growled. "That's it. Milk that dick, Kate. Holy fucking hell, you feel so damn good."

My balls smacked against her ass. Her legs quaked while her pussy quivered around my cock. I gritted my teeth, trying my best to mute my sounds as my balls curled up into my body. And when my cock exploded, I dropped her legs and fell against her body.

Pinning her to the wall as my dick filled her to the brim.

"Oh, yeah."

My face fell to the crook of her neck as she stayed there, suspended helplessly against the wall. My hands gripped her hips, massaging them as she slowly locked her legs back around my body. Her pulsing pussy pushed my cock out from between her legs, and I slowly slid to the floor, taking her with me until she sat in my lap with the water beating aimlessly against her skin.

Dammit, that's exactly what I needed.

"You going to be less of a silent asshole now?" Kate asked.

I snickered. "Sorry for my disposition while we worked out. Work stress is a bitch."

She didn't say anything for a while. But, when she did, I heard the shock laced between her words. "I honestly didn't expect you to even attempt an apology. But, don't think this changes anything."

I shrugged. "Some things change."

She clicked her tongue as if to mock me. "What do you do for work, anyway? I'm sure the stress can't be that bad."

I chuckled. "I'm the CISO of my family's petrol company."

"Oh."

I drew in a deep breath. "So, yeah, there's at least a little bit of stress that comes with the job."

She peered up at me, and I couldn't get enough of that dark emerald stare. "Have you been doing that since you graduated high school?"

I shook my head, still gazing into her eyes. "No."

She scooted out of my lap. "What did you do after high school, then? I mean, not that I care, but you know."

I grinned. "I enlisted."

Her eyebrows rose. "You were in the military?"

I nodded slowly. "Marines. I worked cybersecurity for them, too."

"How long did you serve before you got out?"

I didn't like where this line of questioning was going, so I stood to my feet. I held out my hand for Kate, offering it to her so I could help her up. And to my surprise, she took my hand. But, she was still a bit unsteady on her legs.

"You gonna be okay there, Bambi?" I asked.

She pulled her hand away from mine. "You're the last person to be mocking someone about having weak little chicken legs, especially with the pair you rocked back in high school."

I blinked. "I'm sorry for what I did to you then, too."

Her eyes whipped up to mine. "What did you just say?"

I sighed. "I was a downright asshole to you in high school. The things I did to you simply because you turned me down for dates, it was shameful. I'm not proud of the person I was when I was younger, and I'm sorry you caught the brunt of my actions. Or any of my actions at all."

She blinked. "Well. All right, then. Then—thank you. For —you know, that."

"Not a problem. It's the least I can do."

But, as I stepped out of the shower to make my way into the men's locker room, I felt Kate's wet hand wrap around my wrist.

"You never told me how long you served," she said. Her voice seemed softer, but I wasn't having it.

"Well, you're asking me things you usually ask someone on a date. And this isn't really a date, now, is it?"

She dropped my wrist and scoffed. "That's rich, coming

from the man who just initiated shit that should wait until a date it as least over. But here we are."

I turned around and grinned. "Wanting to know more about the boy you supposedly hate?"

She stumbled over her words. "I just—well—it—you— fuck you, whatever."

I winked. "You kind of already did."

She reached for her washcloth and tossed it at me, soaking my cheek with it as it spread across my skin. She giggled, and the sound tugged a smile across my lips as I slid the hot, wet rag off my face. And when I caught sight of Kate's smile and how beautifully it lit up her face, I couldn't help the words that came flying out of my mouth.

"Why don't you let me take you out for dinner? Then, I won't have any reason not to answer your questions."

Her smile slowly faded away, and her guard flew back up. "Dinner?"

I nodded. "Sure, why not?"

She furrowed her brow softly. "Dinner, with you."

"I mean, I'm not asking for anyone else, if that's what you're wondering."

She snickered. "And you'll answer my questions if I say yes?"

"On my word, I will."

She shrugged. "Okay, then. Dinner, it is. I'm curious about the bully boy who's grown up anyway."

Her words stung, but they were true. I'd been a ruthless fuckwad as a teenager. I had done many things I wasn't proud of and many things I'd carry as heavily weighted guilt until the day I died. But, if taking Kate to dinner was the first step in apologizing for the sorry, pathetic excuse for a human being I'd been in my teenage years, then maybe it was a first step in cultivating the kind of relationship I had wanted with her in the first place.

A want of mind that hadn't seemed to dim after all these years.

"When were you thinking?" Kate asked. Her voice pulled me from my trance.

"I figured we could talk about it during our workout session tomorrow. Unless, of course, I whooped your ass too much today."

She moved the shower curtain over her naked form. "Over my dead body, you did."

I smiled. "Wonderful."

I leaned forward and captured her lips in a soft yet searing kiss. My hand migrated through her hair before I cupped the back of her head, holding her to me so I could taste her for a few seconds longer. Our tongues lingered together lazily as if we had all afternoon to taste and explore each other. But, just like I'd been late pulling away from work, I was late getting back to it.

"See you tomorrow," I whispered against her lips.

I felt her smile. "See you then, big boy."

I grinned at the nickname as I forced myself to pull away, but every ounce of me wanted to charge back into that shower and take her for yet another round. My clothes were soaked, and my shoes squished with every step I took, but fucking hell, it was worth it. I didn't have time to shower, though, so I charged into the men's locker room with my head held high as I gathered my things.

As I walked my happy ass through the gym with water dripping behind me, people looked at me like I had lost my damn mind. I didn't care, though. I had a pending date with who was easily the hottest girl in all of Conroe. Hell, all of Texas. And she had grown into a delectable woman I wouldn't mind enjoying for dessert sometime this weekend. I couldn't wait to finally indulge in the date I'd been dreaming about since I was a horny-ass teenage kid. I couldn't wait to show her the man I had grown into and how that man was completely different from the asshole I'd been back in high school.

And maybe, just maybe, I could squeeze a second date out of her before this was all over.

"Mr. Remington?" The front desk woman—Marjorie—caught my attention as I strolled on by.

"Yep?"

She eyed me curiously. "Everything okay?"

I smiled brightly. "Everything's grand. Could you do something for me, though?"

She leaned against the desk. "Of course. What is it you need?"

I walked over and scribbled my number down on a sheet of torn paper. "Give that to Kate, please. It's pretty sensitive information she's going to need if we're going to keep up our daily appointments."

She slid the piece of paper into her back pocket. "I'll make sure she gets it immediately."

"I appreciate it. You have a good day now."

"You too, Mr. Remington."

I walked out of that gym with my head held high and pride flushing its way through my veins. I felt on top of the world. I felt unstoppable. And I hoped with all my might that Kate called or texted me sometime tonight. I was like a kid in a candy shop, unable to wait until dinner to get another taste of the lusciously forbidden sweets.

And I started counting down the hours in my head until I was in her presence tomorrow for our workout session.

Holy hell, my brothers are never going to believe this shit.

8

Kate

The sun started setting, and the rays pierced through my kitchen window, fervent on making me blind while I munched on my carrots and dip. It had been a long day at the gym, and the last thing I wanted to do was make plans for myself. But, as I stared down at the piece of paper that had his number scrawled onto it, I contemplated calling him.

Or texting him.

Or, just waiting until tomorrow?

"I hate this shit," I murmured.

I picked up another carrot and scooped some hummus onto its tip. I squinted as the sun kept slowly creeping through my small kitchen window, hellbent on forcing me into another room. I wasn't budging, though. Just like I wasn't budging with giving Boone a call.

I just didn't know when to call him.

"Ah, fuck it," I whispered.

I snatched up my phone and dialed his number before putting him on speakerphone. I munched on my food as the phone rang and rang before ultimately shooting me to voice-mail. Perfect. The phone call made the decision for me. All I had to do was leave him a message and—

Oh, he's beeping in.

"Hello. You've reached the voice message of Boone Remington—"

He's still beeping in.

"CISO of Remington—"

Oh, shit. He's not hanging up.

"—a message after the tone—"

"Ugh," I groaned.

I picked up the call beeping in before I left a voice message and drew in a deep breath. Then, once I knew the line had connected, I cleared my throat. "You know, I was just leaving you a voice message."

Boone chuckled, and the sound vibrated my ribcage. "I'd rather speak with you if that's all right."

My heart skipped a beat, and it made me grimace. "So, what are you up to?"

"Bah, nothing much. Just at work."

I blinked. "At this time of the evening?"

"It's barely dinnertime."

"It's a normal end of the workday for most people."

He snickered. "Well, I'm not most people."

"Oh, really. And how do you figure?"

A chair creaked on his end of the phone. "Busy men have busy things to get done on busy schedules. That's how I figure."

I crunched on my carrot and nodded. "Can you say that five times quickly?"

"You know I never back down from a challenge."

I laughed. "Yeah, high school taught me at least that much."

He paused. "Kate, I—"

I waved my hand in the air. "Try it. Five times fast, and no cheating."

"How the hell would you cheat at something like that?"

I shrugged. "I don't know, but you'd find a way. So, try it. Give it your best shot."

I heard him shuffling around. "All right, we'll gloss over the fact that you think I'm a cheater and do this your way. Ready?"

I grinned. "Born ready, baby. Yee yee."

He paused. "I'll also act like you didn't just say 'yee yee.'"

I giggled. "Quit stalling and give it a whirl."

Then, he drew in a deep breath. "Busy men have busy things to get done on busy schedules. Busy men have busy things to get done on dizzy schedules. Busy men have busy things to bet done on busy bedules. Busty men have—"

I broke down laughing. "Busty men!" I threw my head

back and roared with laughter as his chuckles filtered through the phone. I laughed so hard that tears almost came to my eyes, and it gave me pause. I hadn't laughed like that in years. Not since—well, we won't get into that. But, not for a very long time.

And it was with Boone.

But then, my laughter died down, and all that was left was silence. My stomach started growling, and I knew I'd need more sustenance than carrots and hummus to make it shut up. And for a split second, I wondered if Boone would pull away from work to have a quick bite to eat with me.

However, he spoke first. "Look, I can't talk for long, but I have to fly to Vegas for a conference over the weekend, and I leave out tomorrow morning."

My heart sank. "Oh."

"So, any chance I can convince you to come with me?"

I blinked. "Wait. What?"

He snickered. "I know, it's a bit last minute and kind of a weird request. And trust me, I had plans to take you somewhere tomorrow, provided that you said yes. But, now that Ryan isn't going with me anymore, I had to push back my flight to leave out earlier because now I'm a one-man show. Only, the plane tickets and shit I got for Ryan aren't refundable."

I nodded slowly. "Gotcha, gotcha."

"Any chance I can talk you into it? I mean, it's already paid for, so you're covered."

And, of course, my mouth fucked me over as always. "You

bullied me all through high school, you popped into my shower for a quick fuck, and now you want to go to Vegas?"

He paused. "I mean, if you don't want the free trip, that's fine. But, you don't have to spit the past out at me because you can't get over what happened years ago. I'm a completely different person, and I'm trying to show you that. All I'm asking is that you give me a chance."

His words stoked a simmering anger that seemed to take up residence in my gut. And for the life of me, I wanted to tell him to fuck off. I wanted to give him a piece of my mind, let him know just how miserable he had made me, and block his number before banning him from the gym altogether.

However, another part of me figured I deserved a vacation after all the shit life had put me through since graduation. So, I shocked even myself. "You're right."

Boone clicked his tongue. "Well, that's a pleasant surprise."

I shrugged. "I mean, you are right. I'm the one having problems letting go, and I have to admit that a weekend getaway does sound kind of nice. You know, even if it *is* with you."

He chuckled. "So, is that a yes?"

I drew in a deep breath and sealed my fate. "Yes, I'll come with you to Vegas."

"Perfect. I'll pick you up around four in the morning. Our flight leaves at six-thirty."

"Sounds good to me. What should I pack?"

"Oh, you know. A little of this and that. Vegas is always a

little warmer than most areas because of all the lights and the crowds. So, definitely pack to stay as cool as possible."

I nodded slowly. "I'll shoot you my address, then."

"I'll be on the lookout for it."

After solidifying our plans, we said goodbye and hung up the phone. And as I retreated to my bedroom in order to pack a weekend bag, a thought hit me.

This might give me a chance to stick it to Boone finally.

Not in a bad way. But, cheekily. After all, why did he get to get off scot-free after the torturous hell he had put me through simply because "years had passed and he was different?" That didn't matter to me. That didn't cover up all of the derogatory names he'd slung my way and the numerous times he'd tripped me up in the hallways. That didn't cover up the three times he had intentionally broken my glasses and embarrassed me at our senior homecoming dance by "accidentally tripping" and spilling two glasses' worth of punch all down my yellow fucking dress.

He did say it was a business trip.

And what better way to give him a piece of his own medicine than to rack up the bill a bit?

"Not much, though. You don't want to sink him," I murmured.

If hitting Boone in his wallet got him to feel just an inkling of the pain he had put me through, then so be it. It wasn't as if I had any plans to date this fool, after all. For some reason, he had it in his head that we were headed in that direction, and that was on him. I hadn't given him any indication past our moment of screwing around in the shower that I wanted anything even remotely close to that.

"Not my fault if he reads too much into shit," I murmured.

Still, I found myself caring about what I packed. I found myself trying on outfits and seeing how they sat flush against my body. I knew we'd only be gone Friday and Saturday night, but I still wanted to look hot. After all, what good was showing Boone what he couldn't have if he didn't want me in the first place?

"Perfect," I hissed.

After packing up a small suitcase and throwing my toiletries into a bag, I took a long, hot shower. I didn't want to stumble around in the dark at three in the morning in an attempt to clean up before our flight, so I decided to do it beforehand. I let the hot water cascade over my skin, relaxing my aching muscles, and washed away the sweat from my day.

Then—after setting an alarm—I dried off and collapsed into bed.

I tossed and turned, though. Every time my eyes opened, I checked the time to make sure I hadn't missed my alarm; every hour, on the hour, and even a few minutes in between. It was exhausting, not really being able to fall asleep. And I wondered if this meant I'd have a rough weekend trying to sleep in some sleazy-ass hotel with my high school bully in the other room. Because we sure as hell weren't sharing a damn bed.

Nevertheless, at three o'clock in the morning, my alarm

started beeping. I groaned as I reached for it, feeling more sluggish than ever before. I turned off the noise and slid it into my bra before tossing my feet over the edge of the bed. And as I stretched my arms over my head, I felt my back slowly pop into place, one vertebra at a time.

"Oh, yeah. That's the spot," I grunted.

I needed to douse myself in coffee and pack up my chargers. I also had to call in to work. But, after calling out "sick" for my long weekend with Boone, I forced myself to get changed. I stripped off my pajamas and slid into a pair of cotton joggers and a tight tank top. I mean, why not get him drooling beforehand? I threw my hair up into a messy bun and slid into my house shoes, preparing for a very lazy flight into the gambling capital of the US.

But, as I hauled my things down the stairs at three-thirty in the morning, I saw flashing lights waft through the side windows of my front door. I heard a car door shutting as I placed my two bags off to the side. I waited with bated breath as a shadowy figure came onto my porch, blocking out the light from the car's headlights. Then, a thud sounded against my door before Boone's voice came alive.

"I know I'm early, but I come bearing coffee and cheese pastries. You up?"

And I couldn't get the door open quickly enough.

9

Boone

"Holy shit," Kate whispered.

I grinned as I walked through the threshold of the penthouse. "Huh. They really did it up nicely this time."

She cleared her throat. "You mean, it's not this nice all the time? Because I gotta hand it to you guys, this is pretty nice."

I shrugged as I turned left to head down the hallway. "I've been in nicer. Make yourself at home! I need to go set up my office."

The flight into Vegas had been awkward, at best. But, Kate was pretty shocked that we were flying first class. She indulged herself, too. Something I didn't take enough time to do in my world. So, I matched her, purchase for purchase. If she got a hot towel, so did I. If she got a drink, so did I. If she ordered herself a platter of finger foods, I got another one, so we had more things to taste and try together.

But, now that we were in the room, I really had to get set up for work.

I heard her oohing and aahing over all sorts of things, and I tried to block out the sounds. I made my way into the first spare bedroom, heading toward the kitchen, and smiled when I saw a desk in it. The damn thing was the perfect size, and it quickly reminded me why my brothers and I constantly booked this penthouse whenever we flew into Vegas.

So, I started unpacking my tech and hooking up my monitors to all sorts of outlets.

I wanted to be constantly logged in just in case of another attack. And while we hadn't had someone attempt another breach of our systems, I knew it was coming. It was only a matter of time before they tried again. After finally confirming the fact that the hacker hadn't gotten their hands on anything sensitive, my brothers seemed to relax a bit. But not me. Because if that hacker hadn't found what they wanted the first time around, they'd certainly be back whether or not we had more security protocols up and running.

Then, Kate's voice sounded in the doorway. "I'm going to order some room service. You hungry?"

I shrugged. "A steak is always nice."

"Steak and veggies? I can get behind that. What about a surf and turf?"

I shrugged again. "Sure."

"A pitcher of margaritas to go with it?"

I nodded slowly. "Whatever you want."

"How about—"

I waved my hand in the air, cutting her off. "Order whatever you want and get me a steak with, I don't know, something. I need to get this hooked up before I think about anything else."

That was the last I heard of her voice before she backtracked down the hallway. I got my laptop and my extra monitor hooked up and logged into a private internet hub I transported with me whenever we traveled. I made sure the firewalls around that private hub were at least intermediately secured. Not that I thought the hacker would follow me out to Vegas in order to attack us, but one could never be too careful in the world of cybersecurity.

I'd seen some crazy-ass shit in the military.

And dammit, I wouldn't let any of that happen to my family's company.

But, sooner than I would have wished, Kate was back in the room. The smell of fish and chips followed her in before she perched on the bed off to my left and started chowing down on the crispy goodness. I tried to pay attention to the lines of code scrawling across my screen as I tapped into the security system back at the company's headquarters. However, with every tap of my fingers against the keyboard, Kate's eating became louder until it was almost unbearable.

"Can you stop smacking your lips?" I asked.

She giggled. "What? You mean, like this?"

And as if she had balls the size of Zeus's, she started smacking louder, causing my head to turn slowly in her direction.

"I'll put your ass on a plane home if you want to be that coy while I'm working."

She shrugged. "I'm not the one who invited my arch-nemesis to Vegas for a weekend."

I didn't skip a beat. "Well, I'm not the one who still views anyone as a nemesis. Get your head out of high school, Kate."

Out of the corner of my eye, I saw my laptop screen flashing red, and it ripped me out of my angry trance. I whipped my head back toward my workstation and started typing away as quickly as I could, watching as one line of code scrawled through hundreds in the blink of an eye.

"An auto-crawler," I glowered.

Kate slid off the bed. "Is everything okay?"

"*Shh*, let me concentrate."

I leaned toward my screens and tried to chase down the stupid little bug. The issue with something like this was that it moved so quickly that it barely gave me time to track where the hell it had come from in the first place. That meant no cornering it, no reverse-engineering it, and certainly no locking it out.

"Fuck, fuck, fuck, fuck, fuck," I hissed.

Kate bent over my shoulder. "What can I do?"

I felt my voice growing. "Will you just leave me alone while I work, please?"

I knew yelling at her was wrong. I knew it the second my

voice sounded against my own damn ears. But, I had an emergency of epic proportions going on in front of me, and she was concerned with distracting me just to get back at me for shit that had happened years ago when we were fucking kids. I didn't have time for that nonsense. Did I owe her an apology? Of course, I did. That was part of the reason why I had invited her to Vegas, to begin with.

Hopefully, to start a trail of good deeds that might amount to the kind of apology that she deserved.

"Fine, whatever," she murmured.

A video call came in from Wyatt, and it cut off my ability to shoot back at her, which was probably for the best. We were both jet-lagged, tired as hell, and needed naps.

But, I picked up the video call anyway, not caring where Kate was standing.

"Wyatt, I know, and I'm on it. But, it's an auto-crawler this time. So, it'll take—"

His voice sounded harsh. "Who the fuck is that behind you?"

I didn't bother looking at his face. "What?"

"That? Over there! I see a fucking lady leg on the bed."

I sighed. "That's Kate."

"Kate, who? What the fuck is going on?"

"My big mistake for the weekend, with the way things are going right now. Don't worry about it."

Kate scoffed. "Fuck you, too, Boone."

Wyatt clicked his tongue. "Well, can you get her out of the —wait a second. I know that voice."

Kate sighed. "Hi, Wyatt."

I peeked over at the video just enough to see Wyatt gawk. "Holy fuck, that's *Kate* Kate. The one who kept rejecting you in high school?"

She got up from the bed and stood over my shoulder again. "The one and only."

I groaned. "Can you get out of the room so I can deal with this sensitive situation with my business partner?"

"You mean, the blinking red screen your brother's about to lay into you for? I kind of want to see that."

I barked at her. "Out! Now!"

And when I focused back on my laptop, my monitor started blinking red. Meaning that the auto-crawler was done with one system and had hopped to another.

"You guys will have to start unplugging again," I murmured.

Kate slammed the bedroom door behind her, and Wyatt chuckled. "I never know what possesses you to go to Vegas. I hate that place. Way too many people, and it reeks of sex and drugs. But, why you wanted to take Kate with you is beyond me."

I growled. "Did you hear me, Wyatt? Be prepared to unplug."

"You know there are other ways to punish yourself for the fact that you're still alive, right?"

I stared directly into the laptop camera and glared. "One more move, and I'll release every security protocol I have and let them have at it."

Wyatt waved his hand in the air. "What do you need to help with this?"

I hunkered down and continued typing away. "Some goddamn answers."

Wyatt had definitely gotten soft on me since meeting Bella. Don't get me wrong; I thought Bella was lovely. But, all of my brothers had gotten a bit softer around the edges since becoming family men and all that bullshit. I needed sharks playing with me while we were working. I needed the old Wyatt who would've pioneered the investigation into this himself, not this nonchalant, joke-making fiend he had turned into.

"Have you fucked her yet?" Wyatt asked.

I threw my hands into the air. "Does no one want to shut up while I try to do my job?"

"I'll take that as a 'no' since you're still so high-strung."

I slammed my fists against my keyboard. "Unplug everything. Unplug it now!"

The red blinking screens mocked me as Wyatt started placing phone calls, and a few seconds later, our video call went blank. I chewed on the inside of my cheek as the auto-crawler jumped from page to page, devouring everything in sight. If steam could've come out of my ears, there would've been a damn mushroom cloud of it hanging over the fucking hotel.

And after I unplugged everything on my end, I plugged it back in so I could get to work. "Time to figure out who you are," I growled.

This time it took me damn near three hours to track down an IP address, which meant whoever was behind this had come into this attack ready to take on whatever security system I could throw at it. And that wasn't good. That meant the person on the other end was evolving, and judging by how stuck in his ways Mr. Blanchard was, I had a hard time believing it could be him doing all of this, wreaking all of this havoc in a company that had netted him millions.

But, when it was all said and done, I extracted the information I needed in order to obtain an IP address that was easy to back-trace. And my face paled when the identification behind the address popped up.

"What's with the face?" Wyatt asked.

I jumped at the sound of his voice. "How the fuck—"

"Hey, you're the one who set all of our Skype calls to pick up automatically if any one of us calls the other twice within thirty seconds."

I looked over at him as I slumped back into my chair. "I got it."

"You got what?"

I raked my hands through my hair. "Another physical address for this IP that infiltrated our system."

He blinked. "Well. Let me have it. What's the address now?"

I ran my hands down my face. "It's still Mr. Blanchard's home address."

It didn't make sense, and yet all of the information was there. I was staring at it, and I knew damn good and well I hadn't gotten anything wrong in the process. Not the first time around, and certainly not this time.

Wyatt's sigh pulled me out of my shocked trance. "Get me the information I need, and I'll pass it onto the police."

I licked my lips. "Actually, I think I have a better way of going about this, if you have a second to listen."

He leaned toward the camera. "All right, you have my attention."

And as I rattled off what was on my mind, it didn't even occur to me what Kate was doing. Or where she had gotten off to. Or what kind of mood she was in. It didn't even occur to me to check in on her as I lost myself in all of the technical jargon and bullshit that had consumed my life. So, maybe that meant Wyatt was right after all.

Maybe I was punishing myself for the fact that I was still alive when my men weren't.

❧ 10 ❧

Kate

I stormed out of Boone's room and locked myself in my own. I had never felt so disrespected, so disregarded, and so pissed off in all my life. No. No, no. I was more than pissed off. I was—I was—

Whatever the hell I was, it was more than pissed.

If there were a word that meant "more than pissed," I needed to know it. And if there weren't a word for it, then I needed to come up with one because the angry energy coursing through my veins that caused me to chew on the skin of my lips until they bled needed a name. It had made a home inside the carcass of a body that once knew how to live life.

"Fucking asshole of a human being," I hissed. I dropped

myself into a plush chair in the corner and set my food off to the side. "Don't know why the fuck I thought he could change."

I scooped up the remote control and turned on the wall-mounted flatscreen television.

"I hope he chokes on his keyboard when he tries to chew it out; he loves it so much," I glowered.

I couldn't believe that he had yelled at me like that. Spoken to me like that. Treated me like a piece of trash he had dragged in from off the street on the heel of his boot. Tears of anger streaked my cheeks as I gripped the remote control. I felt the buttons digging into my skin, imprinting their pattern against my palm. I vibrated with a need for release. I wanted to scream and throw things around and listen to glass plates shatter into a billion pieces.

Maybe then I won't be the only thing broken in this penthouse.

And, of course, his rude-ass brother had to bear witness to it all. Poor Kate Riley, the idiotic bitch who thought she could one-up Boone Remington. I should've known better than to accept his invitation to something like this. Now, I was away from home, cooped up in a place that wasn't mine, using money that wasn't mine, while the boy who had tortured me for years mocked me and yelled at me like some useless dog in front of his equally treacherous brother.

Why the hell am I here again?

It was supposed to be my weekend to get back at him. My weekend to level the playing field and make Boone understand—once and for all—how he had really made me feel. But all he was doing was winning. All he was doing was showing me exactly the kind of disgusting person I had always pegged him to be. And for once, I wondered whether I could out-disgust the man who had practically trademarked the word.

Guess the Remington Brothers aren't so gentlemanly after all.

However, after eating my food and watching reruns of *Golden Girls* on television, I grew bored. I was in Vegas, for crying out loud. Why the hell was I cooped up in a hotel room? I mean, yeah, it was more than a hotel room. It was a penthouse suite with floor-to-ceiling windows in the living room, four bedrooms, four bathrooms, a balcony with a private pool and hot tub, and amenities so great and grand that it would make even billionaires drool and go weak in the knees. But that didn't mean I wanted to be inside of it with Boone.

So, I decided to get dressed. I took a shower to wash the first-class flight off my skin, I hopped into a summer dress with a matching pair of flats, and I decided to make a run at his credit card. This resort we were in had everything, and every charge was connected to the card on file. Which meant that all I had to do was stroll into the spa, start ordering services, and make sure to tip as wildly as possible.

And that's exactly what happened.

If Boone was going to be attached to that makeshift office of his, then I was going to head out and make some memo-ries. I headed down to the spa, two floors beneath us, and walked right up to the front counter, ready to have myself a nice little spa day. I'd never had one before, so I wasn't sure what to expect. But, I decided to book a battery of splurges I knew I'd never be able to afford by myself.

A facial.

A two-hour massage with a seaweed wrap.

A mud soak, whatever the hell that was.

A nice cut and dye for my hair.

Nails and toes, of course.

And to cap off my splurge day, a nice meal at the restaurant just off the main lobby downstairs.

But, once I got back up to the room somewhere around seven in the evening, I found Boone standing at the massive living room windows. With his hands clasped behind his back. And as I stepped off the private elevator in my summer dress with matching flats, he turned to face me.

"I was wondering when you'd be back," he said.

I drew in a sobering breath to calm myself down. "How'd the rest of work go?"

He walked toward me and stood so close that I felt his body heat reaching out for me. "Just to let you know, you're racking up the company card. Not my personal card."

I tried not to look as disappointed as I felt. "I figured as much."

He scoffed, shaking his head. "You really are still living back in high school, aren't you?"

That's it. I've had enough. "You know, Remington, you made my life a living fucking hell back then. I cried to my mother more nights than I care to count about pulling me out and homeschooling me because of you. The only time I ever contemplated suicide was during high school. And now, you're pissed off at me for being childish? After I literally begged my parents to move to get away from you?"

I looked up at him and saw his stone-cold eyes peering down at me. And when he didn't speak, I decided to continue.

"You really are a piece of work. You tortured me because I wouldn't go on a date with you. You filled my locker with rotten fruit, vegetables, and other things that forced my parents to pay for new books when we didn't even have the money for me to buy new shoes, and you're pissed because I took a spa day to myself after you raised your voice at me and tossed me out of some room like a piece of trash? After you invited me here in the first place? Seriously, Boone?"

His eye twitched, and I figured I had hit a nerve. But instead of yelling at me or telling me to get a cab to the airport, he said the one phrase that let me know he'd never change. That let me know he'd never be the boy everyone always thought he was.

"Grow up, Kate. Multiple lives have been lived and lost since we were in high school. So, if you can't buck it up and suck it up, then just leave me out of it and go do your thing. The company can stomach the loss in funds if that's really what you need to get your rocks off."

I clenched my fists at my sides. "Yeah, well, you're too late with that lesson. My brother dying already taught me that, you arrogant son of a bitch."

I turned to walk away from him, but he reached out for my arm. He spun me around, and I prepared myself for a fight, readying my arms to fly at a second's notice. He had a massive jawline, and I had very good aim with my fists. But, then I watched the way his stone-cold eyes softened.

And it caught me off-guard.

"Your brother died?" he asked.

I grimaced. "I'm not talking about this."

"When did he die, Kate?"

I shot him a look. "I said, I'm not talking about this."

He sighed. "I'm sorry, Kate. I had no idea."

I snorted. "Whatever. I'm going home."

I ripped away from him and stormed off to my room. I wasn't sure what the hell this weekend was supposed to be, but clearly, it wouldn't amount to what either of us had planned for it to become. And the last thing I wanted to do was spend more time in the presence of a man I wished would have died instead of my brother.

So, I started throwing my things into my suitcase.

"Kate, stop."

Boone's voice fell on deaf ears as I gathered my toiletries from the bathroom.

"Kate, please. I'm asking you kindly to stop."

I tossed my toiletries onto the bed. "Maybe try actually *being* nice for once in your pathetic life."

"I get it, okay? I'm a dick. I'm a bastard."

I scoffed. "For starters. Now, buzz off so I can find a cab that'll take me—"

He gripped my shoulders and forced me to look into his eyes. "Kate."

I cleared my throat to keep from crying. "What?"

"I really am sorry for how I spoke with you earlier. You're right. I never should've yelled at you like that. I should've kindly asked you to leave so I could work on what was happening, and I didn't do that. I've never been good at emotions while under pressure, and I'm sorry it backlashed onto you."

My eyes danced between his. "You're being serious."

He nodded. "As a heart attack."

I swallowed hard. I wasn't sure what to make of the apology, but it at least sounded genuine. And just like that, I felt myself softening toward Boone. I felt the need to take him into my arms, hug him, and tell him that everything would be all right, which made me feel so disappointed in myself. Was that how desperate I had become for a man's affection? So desperate that some half-assed apology that had nothing to do with the original issue made me warm toward him?

You're losing it, Kate. Stay strong.

"I appreciate it," I said.

His hands slid down my arms, squeezing them softly on the journey. "I had no idea about Sebastian. Kate, I'm so fucking sorry. I had no idea he passed away."

I shrugged off his touch. "He knew the risks when he joined the army."

"As a man who once enlisted into the marines, I can guarantee you that isn't true."

I wanted to slap him across his face.

Maybe he should've come home instead of you.

The second the words trampled their way into my mind, it shocked me back to reality. This was where my anger had gotten me. This was where holding on to all of that residual frustration had landed me. I was standing in front of Boone Remington on a Vegas weekend trip he didn't need me to pay for, and I was actively attempting to make his life a living nightmare.

Is this really the person I want to be?

"How about we make a deal?" Boone asked.

His voice pulled me from the recesses of my mind. "What kind of deal?"

He took a step back. "I'll take you out for drinks to try to make up to you for today, and then I'll personally see to it that you have a comfortable and safe flight home tomorrow if you still want to leave after you sleep."

I shook my head. "I don't think this situation needs alcohol, Boone."

"What if I throw in food with the drinks?"

I quirked my eyebrow. "Like... a date?"

He chuckled. "I was thinking more about dinner with a show of some sort. You know, just to get us out from behind these walls so we can experience something that isn't anger or work."

I turned the offer around in my head. "It does sound kind of nice."

"I know how much you like live music, and there are plenty of last-minute concerts with dinner and drinks we can book."

I tilted my head off to the side. "And if I still want to leave tomorrow, I can?"

He nodded. "I'll even help you pack and get downstairs."

I grinned. "Then, I guess I better put on something that screams 'Vegas nightlife.'"

And when he smiled, my heart stilled in my chest.

"I'll see you here by the elevator in an hour, then."

I nodded. "See you in an hour."

11

Boone

I opened the car door for Kate. "Your taxi, milady."

She giggled. "You're insane; quit doing that."

I slipped in beside her. "Quit doing what, mibeauty?"

She kept giggling. "Talking like you're some sort of sophisticated pirate."

I leaned toward her a bit. "Arrr-ye vast lady Kraken. What does a lad have to do to get ye-lone for the night?"

She barked with laughter. "What the hell was that?"

I laughed along with her. "I honestly have no clue."

Our driver's voice pierced through the laughter. "Where to, sir?"

I cleared my throat. "Dinner and a show, please, at The Colosseum."

"I cannot believe I'm about to go see the queen herself, live and in person. Oh, I can't wait!"

I kept my eyes forward. "It'll be new for both of us. I've actually never taken in a Vegas music show before."

She gasped. "You're kidding. You talk about Vegas like you've been here a million times, though."

I chuckled. "Let's just say I'm more of a magic show person."

"Wait a second, you didn't tell me they had magic shows here."

I peeked over at her. "If you choose to stay tomorrow night as well, I don't have any issues taking you out to see one."

Her eyes met mine, and I had a hard time not letting them drop. I mean, her skin-tight dress was enough to make any man salivate, especially since it clung to her luscious curves. Her smooth legs glistened with body glitter, and the effervescent smell of flowers and bubblegum pouring from the nape of her neck made me want to bury my nose against her skin and never come up for air. With her strawberry-blond hair tumbling well past her shoulders and her dark-green eyes twinkling with the lights of Vegas, she was easily the most beautiful woman I'd ever laid my eyes on.

I guess some things never change.

And while part of me knew she was trying to get to me, I didn't care. I knew what personal loss felt like, and she did as well. The fact that I didn't know her brother had died showed me just how much I had checked out of Conroe after I had lost my men on the battlefield. And that was no one's fault but my own.

She held onto the same kind of anger I did.

And maybe—just maybe—we could help each other with that.

I had to turn my eyes away, though. I let them fall out the back window of the taxi as I stared at the hazy lights passing us by in a blurry whirl. I felt my cock swelling against my suit pants, and I knew I was in trouble this evening. Kate looked delectable enough to eat, and part of me wanted to bypass this "dinner and a show" altogether just so I could get her back up to my room—and have my way with her.

"Ah! We're here!" Kate squealed.

I grinned. "Here, let me get out and get your—"

She opened her door too quickly, though. "Come on, Boone! We need to get good seats."

I wanted to tell her that our seats were already reserved, but seeing her so happy and excited wasn't something I wanted to ruin. I paid the taxi driver and tipped him accordingly, then slid out of the back seat and fastened the button of my suit jacket.

Then, I stepped up onto the curb and offered her my arm.

"Don't mind if I do," she said with a smile.

And when her arm fell against my own, her heat breathed new life into my tired bones.

Her eyes widened when the ticket-taker ushered us over

to a VIP section, but when she saw how vibrant and private our little alcove was, she practically gushed. She raced over to the microfiber couch and flopped against it, kicking off her heels as if she were at home. She looked so comfortable that I took a page out of her book and slipped out of my patent leather shoes. Then, I eased myself onto the couch beside her as a waitress came up to our side.

"Would you two like a menu? Or do you know what you'd like to drink?" she asked.

I chewed on the inside of my cheek. "Uh, I'll take a nice homebrew if you have any."

The waitress smiled. "We have two in-house beers we make on sight: an IPA and a stout."

I nodded. "I'll have the stout."

Kate leaned over me. "And I'll have the IPA. That way, we can both taste a bit, yeah?"

I blinked. "Wait, you're a beer drinker?"

She giggled. "Always have been, always will be. Even back during high school, if you can believe it."

My jaw unhinged as the waitress left with our drink orders. "Geeky, nerdy little Kate from high school with glasses as thick as my dick drank when she wasn't supposed to?"

She rolled her eyes. "Of course, everything routes back to your dick."

I cupped my hand over my mouth. "Stop the press! Scandal at Conroe High! Stop the press, I tell ya!"

She nudged me as laughter almost robbed her of her voice. "Stop. I can't—I'm gonna pee. Boone, I'm gonna pee."

I looked down at her as she laid her head against my chest, trying to catch her breath, she was laughing so hard. And before I knew it, I was laughing right along with her. We kept laughing and picking at one another until our drinks arrived. We quickly looked at menus before I ordered us one of every-thing. I mean, the menu wasn't that extensive. Two salads, two soups, three entrees, four kinds of dessert, and something called a "seafood extravaganza appetizer."

"Oh, man. They're going to have to roll me out of here. This IPA is out of this world. Here, try some."

Kate handed me her drink, and I took a sip of it before I gazed longingly down into my stout.

"I don't even know if I should drink this now," I murmured.

Kate snickered. "Just try a sip. Trust me, if you don't like it, you can have my IPA, and I'm sure I'll down it."

I peered over at her. "That a promise?"

She held up her drink. "I'll toast to it."

We clinked our glasses together before she watched me like a hawk. I readied myself for the stout to be one tier short of disappointing after having a sip of the flavorful IPA she had in her hand. But, the second the dark beer hit the tip of my tongue, I stood to my feet.

"Uh-uh," I said.

Kate stood. "What? What's wrong?"

I held it up in the air. "This is mine, and you can't have it."

She scoffed. "Just let me have a sip. That's what we said we were going to do, right?"

I shook my head. "If you sip this, you won't stop."

She reached up with her hand. "We can always order another one, you idiot. Come on. Just one sip, I promise. Okay?"

I playfully glared at her. "Promise?"

She batted her eyelashes at me. "On my body, Mr. Boone."

I groaned. "I hate you."

She smiled. "I know. Now, let me try a little bit."

I handed her the drink and watched her take a sip. But, just like I thought, that sip turned into a chug. I went to grab the beer away from her, trying to save some for myself. However, she kept backing up with each step I took toward her until her shoulders pressed against the outer glass bubble of our cozy, private VIP alcove.

"Kate," I said sternly.

She took another pull. "You're right. This is delectable."

I wrapped my hand around the glass beneath her hand. "Let go. Now."

Her eyes held mine. "What's the magic word?"

Seeing her lips move as they curled around the edge of the glass, sent my cock pulsing with need. I had to put some space between us; otherwise, she'd feel the intrusion sooner rather than later. Her body drew me closer as I gripped the beer glass tighter. I peered down into her eyes from my perched position, watching her cheeks tint with a beautiful color that I wanted to see her entire body flushed with.

"The only magic word around here," I said, "is the one that gets you out of this dress for me. But since that word doesn't exist, I'll settle for, 'let go of my beer before I cut you off.'"

She drew in a shaky breath before she grinned. "You don't have to be so harsh about it."

I winked as I pulled the glass away from her. I tipped back what was left and drained the cup before I ripped her IPA from her hand. She balked and scoffed as I threw that one back as well, filling my stomach with about as much alcohol as she had stolen from me.

Then, when the waitress came in with our seafood extravaganza, I told her to keep the beers coming before I ushered Kate back to the couch.

"You cut well in a suit, you know," she said.

The waitress brought us refreshed beers, and I leaned back against the couch. "You don't look half bad yourself."

"Oh, trust me, I already know that."

Ugh. I loved confidence in a woman, and Kate had that shit in droves. I wanted to find a way to get the conversation flowing well between the two of us again. I didn't want to resort to having fights with her just to get her to converse with me. But, before I found a way to do that, Celine herself came out onstage, and Kate squealed so shrilly I thought the glass was going to rupture.

So, I decided to lose myself in the show.

Kate and I shared food and downed beers as quickly as we could drink them. And about halfway through the show, when the lights came up to show everyone to the restroom, I knew I wouldn't be able to stand without stumbling.

"You know," Kate said as she leaned against me, "I sometimes wish I could go back to high school, as much as I hated it."

I grinned. "And why's that?"

She sighed. "I'd get to see Sebastian that way."

I winced. "I'm sorry for the shit I put you through back then. You didn't deserve any of it."

She shrugged. "Eh, it's in the past. I shouldn't be dwelling on it."

"I still owe you an apology."

She nodded slowly. "You do. Or, you did, at least. Apology accepted."

"Just like that?"

She leaned up and turned toward me before she hiccuped. "Just like that. My brother would've wanted it that way. He always thought you were a 'diamond in the rough.'"

"Sebastian was always trying to help me through math, you know. Always trying to get me to go to his tutoring sessions."

Her smile faded a bit. "Yeah. I think he considered you a special project or something like that."

I chuckled. "I would've been a tough one back then."

"Why were you such an asshole, by the way?"

I sipped my beer and shrugged. I didn't want to break the ice too quickly between us, but I enjoyed how the conversation flowed, even if we were four beers in and clouded by alcohol. Still, she kept pressing, and I figured that I owed her at least a few answers.

So, I gave in. "I guess I was an asshole because I felt useless."

She balked. "What?"

I licked my lips. "Yeah, can you believe that? High school football star, wrestling star, cross-country star, and I felt fucking useless."

She turned her entire body to face me. "But why? Who convinced you that you were useless?"

I shrugged as I gazed out among the sea of heads, making their way back to their seats. "Myself, I guess. I don't know, I saw all of my brothers graduating and going on to help with positions in the family company, and I didn't want anything to do with that shit. I wanted to make my own way, and I guess I lost myself in that attempt. It seemed the only thing we had in common was our love of the rodeo."

Her hand fell against my thigh. "Boone, look at me."

I peered over at her. "Yeah?"

She squeezed my thigh. "You did make your own way. You didn't do things the way your brothers did. You didn't do things the way people from small towns always do things."

"Still ended up at the family's company and identifying with the Remingtons and the Rocking R Ranch, though."

"Except now you want to be there, right?"

I paused. "Yeah, you're right."

She shrugged. "Then, you made your own way. You carved your own path until you were ready to be where you were meant to be. And that takes some serious balls."

She was right. It did. And when the show started back up,

I felt her lean against me. We tanked through food and desserts and beer like we had bottomless stomachs, and as the show wound down to a close, Kate needed to hold onto me in order to get out the front doors.

I felt powerful, feeling her cling to me. I felt useful again as we both stumbled around. Despite my overly drunken state, I kept an eye out for anyone or anything that might try to hurt Kate, and it felt like I had a purpose again. But, I saw no taxis in sight after the show.

"Where's our driver?" she asked.

Her words slurred together, and I drew in a sobering breath. Well, an attempt at a sobering breath anyway. "Uh, don't know. I think they're bussing lots of people home right now."

"Does Vegas have an Uber?"

I snickered. "Let's go find somewhere to sit down and we can find out."

I heard my own words slurring as we stumbled across the road. I wanted to scoop her into my arms, but dammit, I was unsteady enough as it was on my own two feet. Cars honked as we walked across the road, leaning against each other to stay upright. And when we dropped down onto a set of concrete steps, I looked up at the sign casting an ethereal glow over us.

"Uncle Dave's Wedding Chapel?" I asked.

Kate gasped and turned around. "It's a Vegas wedding chapel! Oh, man. I've been told you've never been to Vegas until you've been inside one of those things."

I chuckled. "That so?"

She nodded vigorously. "Yep. I mean, not like I'll ever know what a wedding feels like. I can't stop working long enough to date. But, I've been told some crazy—" *Hiccup!*

Trust me, I'm a workaholic, too.

I watched her swallow hard, trying her best not to puke before she kept talking. "Crazy stories. I think. Yeah, stories."

She leaned against me, and I felt the world tilting off its axis. I squinted my eyes to try to right the world, but it didn't do much. I placed my cheek against her head and heard her hiccuping, trying to keep her food down inside of her stomach. And when a warm, gusty wind laced with cocaine and cigarette smoke picked up, I covered my nose.

"Let's go inside," I murmured.

Kate lifted her head. "What's that smell?"

I helped her to her feet before I stumbled, almost taking her to the ground. She giggled with delight as we both used each other to stand, and together we made our way into the chapel. The smell of drugs and smoke gave way to the stale smell of sweat and desperation, but the lobby had comfy-looking couches that I wanted to sprawl out on.

And after Kate and I crashed down against the cushions, I felt her looking at the profile of my face as I tried to focus my eyes.

"Do you ever date?" she asked.

I lobbed my head over to look at her. "Nah. I work too much."

She patted my knee. "Preachin' to the choir, my man."

I snorted. "My man. All I ever wanted to hear you say in high school was that I was your man."

She shoved me playfully. "Got a shitty way of showing that."

My head lobbed over to the other side. "Hey, listen. You want a story to take home to your friends?"

"It's funny that you think I have friends."

"All right, you're boss?"

She paused. "I'm listening. Whatcha got in mind?"

And when I finally moved my head back in her general direction, I felt a smile lift my cheeks. "Doozy stories, right?"

She nodded lazily. "Right."

I held out my hand. "So, let's make one of our own. Let's have ourselves a fake-ass wedding and freak everyone out."

She gasped. "Yeah! We can get pictures taken and put them up online."

I barked with laughter. "We can get cheap rings and really shine them up to make them look real."

She stood to her feet before she stumbled back into my lap. "We can even post romantic pictures of bubbles in a tub with rose petals and shit. Really do it up and make people think this has turned into a big ol' honeymoon."

I scooped her into my arms and tried to pick her up before I stumbled and fell back onto the couch. We both busted out laughing, and never in my life had my cheeks hurt so much from smiling so big. It was a great idea, though. One for the ages, if anyone asked me about it. It was something I could really use to throw my brothers for a loop, especially since they always seemed to prank me and get away with it.

So, once I found the strength to stand to my feet, I held out my hand and watched Kate slip her palm against mine.

"Kate Riley?"

She scooted to the edge of the couch. "Oh yes, Boone?"

I snorted. "Will you fake-marry me and be my fake-wife so we can fake-out everyone who pisses us off?"

Then, she stood to her feet and stumbled against me for support. "I'd love nothing more."

And the smallest part of me wondered if she'd let me have a shot at rocking her world back at the penthouse during our fake-wedding night after we got fake-married.

12

Kate

As the infamous song, "The Wedding March" started playing on an old, scratched-up record, I curled my lips over my teeth. I tried my hardest not to laugh as I walked down the aisle, holding a bouquet of dilapidated, fake flowers in my hand to match the toilet paper veil I had hastily put together in the bathroom that needed a bit more attention than it was getting. Watching Boone giggle at the end of the aisle like a little schoolgirl sent me into a laughing frenzy. By the time I got to the altar, "The Wedding March" was skipping so incessantly it sounded like the damn recording was trying to clap for us.

And I couldn't contain myself. "Can someone cut that off? It sounds so weird," I said through my giggling.

Boone let his head fall back as he hung onto me to stay upright. "Anything for my bride!"

I roared with laughter as I leaned against him, propping myself up since the alcohol we threw back seemed to go straight to my legs. At one point in time, my veil started shedding, and I watched as little cheap-as-hell toilet squares fell against his pristine and shining shoes. I barely got through the absolutely ridiculous jumble of words the old man kept rattling off as we stood in front of him. But then, he spoke the words into existence.

"Have you written your vows?" he asked.

Boone wiped at his tears. "Yes, yes, yes. Oh, yes. I have plenty of vows. Ready for this?"

I looked up at him. "Better make it good if ya wanna get laid, buddy."

He snorted. "All right, here goes. I, Boone Remington, promise not to put rotten fruit in your locker for as long as I live."

I cackled. "And I, Kate Riley, promise never to have a locker in my life, so I don't have to punch you in the balls when you break your promise."

We teetered on our feet as we slid the five-buck wedding rings onto our fingers. The damn things were practically made of tin foil, but that shit didn't matter. None of this was real, anyway! And as we marched back up the aisle, with Boone trying to pick me up and failing along the way, we laughed our asses right back out onto the bustling, bright street of Vegas before finally hailing a cab to take us back to the hotel.

"Congratulations on your nuptials," our driver murmured.

I peeked over at Boone and almost fell apart, laughing again. "Ah, thanks."

Boone winked at me. "Never thought I'd finally nail her, but it looks like I just might tonight."

My head fell back with effortless laughter, but I couldn't deny the heat that pooled between my legs. I blamed it on the alcohol and let that be that, but when we got back up to the penthouse we were occupying for the weekend, I found that I wanted a repeat of our shower escapades. I wanted to feel his body against mine once more. I wanted to grip his hair as his tongue ventured between my thighs.

I wanted to enjoy him before we woke up from our drunken stupors and realized how idiotic we were being.

Before I knew it, I woke up the next morning with my clothes still on and my body resting against Boone's... on the couch. Somehow, we had gotten from the chapel to the hotel and managed to stumble inside and drop onto the deep-sofa couch that could have easily slept four different people. I stretched my arms over my head and kicked off my heels. I licked my lips and grimaced at the feeling of wadded-up paper against my lips.

Then, I felt Boone shift before he groaned. "Holy hell."

I drew in a deep breath. "I feel like I got hit by a damn bus."

He chuckled. "Can't hold your beer?"

I slowly pressed myself upright. "Says the guy complaining about moving."

"I didn't complain."

I rolled my eyes. "You groaned. That might as well be complaining in caveman speak."

I felt the couch shift before Boone's footfalls started stumbling away from me, and I curled up on the cushions. I reached around until I found a blanket and pulled it over my head, ready to sleep the rest of the day away. If he wanted me in any sort of shape to fly out early in the morning on Sunday, then I needed a day to get some beauty rest after the insanity of last night.

But I should have known I wouldn't have been so damn lucky.

"Fuck!"

The harshness of Boone's voice caused me to throw the covers off my head. I stood to my bare feet and held on to any wall I could find as I followed the sound of his cursing. I closed one eye and squinted the other, trying not to puke on myself as I emerged into the pristine kitchen.

And when I saw him sitting at the breakfast nook, I walked over to him. "What is it?" I asked.

He didn't answer me, though. All he did was hold out his hands as if the evidence were right in front of me. And sure enough, it was.

"Oh. My. God. Is that—"

Boone cut me off. "Yep."

My heart stilled in my chest. "But, we said—"

He nodded. "We did."

I pointed to the middle of the paper. "But, that's—a marriage certificate?"

Boone stood to his feet. "I need to go make some phone calls."

I swallowed hard as I dropped down into the seat he had just left. I pulled the manilla envelope toward me that had Boone's name on it and eased the rest of the papers out from their depths. There were pictures of all things from last night. The two of us, drunk off our rockers, trying to walk up the aisle of some musty, crusty wedding chapel in the middle of the night.

"Toilet paper veil?" I whispered to myself.

I put the pictures down after promising myself to burn them and looked back at the certificate of marriage. My trembling fingertips gripped it and held it up to my face as if some watermark would magically show me that this damned thing was fake. But, the harder I looked, the more legitimate it appeared.

And panic flushed its way through my veins.

The wedding last night wasn't fake.

I looked over at Boone and found him staring at his cell phone with a blank expression on his face. It didn't look like he was all there, so I snapped my fingers. He didn't hear the snapping, but he sure as hell heard my whistling. And when he jolted out of his trance, he quickly came to sit in front of me.

He drew in a deep breath. "All right, here's what we're going to do."

I reached out and placed my shaking hand against his forearm. "Are you okay, Boone?"

His eyes slowly met mine. "Yeah. Why wouldn't I be?"

"I lost you there for a second. I want to make sure you're all right."

He shrugged and leaned back, pulling away from my touch. "Yeah, I'm good. I'm always good. You know this."

I knew he was lying to me, but I didn't have the energy to sift through it. Not that he was worth that energy in the first place. I wanted to blame this on him. I wanted to ask him how the hell he was so reckless as to not inform the chapel owners that we had essentially paid them to play pretend. But I knew it was just as much my fault as it was his.

I'd had the capability to speak up last night, and I hadn't.

"I'll make us some coffee," Boone murmured.

I nodded as I looked back down at the papers. "Good. That sounds like a good idea."

He walked over to the kitchen counter. "If you look at the receipt they included, I apparently bought some sort of 'honeymoon package' with these cheap-ass rings."

I drew in sobering breaths to stop the world from spinning around me as I rifled through the papers, finally coming across the sale's receipt. And right there, in plain print, were four ticketed items: one wedding ceremony, two-thirty dollar rings—which weren't even worth the paper the money was printed on—and something called a "deluxe honeymoon package."

I grinned. "Cheaping out on the rings to give me a nice honeymoon, Remington?"

He didn't respond, though. And when I looked down at the bottom of the receipt, the words that flew out at me caused me to run to the kitchen sink and puke up my guts.

Purchases final. No refunds accepted.

Holy shit, I'm fucking married.

❧ 13 ❧

Boone

Every time I looked at my watch, it was a different time. And not just a slightly different time, but I was losing massive gaps. Every time my brain started to focus, it came back around to the one glaring thing I couldn't rip out of the recesses of my mind.

I was married to Kate Riley.

How the fuck did this happen? How in the hell could they have misinterpreted me so badly? I tried to remember back to the exact moment when I told the old man officiating that this wasn't real. It was just something to occupy our time until some taxis were freed up. But dammit, I couldn't remember past the show ending last night.

"I'm never drinking like that again," I groaned.

I walked around in a haze. One minute, Kate was in the kitchen with me, looking over the papers that had been delivered, and the next minute, the coffee pot had turned off, and the black liquid was lukewarm at best. So, I decided to bury myself in work until the urge to call up the chapel and curse them into hell itself dissipated.

"Shit, it's almost three," I murmured.

Three in the afternoon and all I'd done was walk around in a haze. I wanted to smash something. I wanted to break someone's face. But, I knew the closest I could get to that kind of outlet was exercising.

And I couldn't get into my gear quickly enough.

Thank fuck, the resort had a really nice gym on the third floor, and I had every intention of using those free weights until my legs fucking buckled beneath me. Because that was the only way I wouldn't wind back up at that chapel after I got some food into my system and this hangover finally dissipated.

Only my legs not functioning would keep me from going over there and cursing out two lovely, elderly individuals.

As I came out of my bedroom, though, I heard the faintest sniffle. It caught my ear and rooted me to my place, and that's when I heard it. The soft sounds of Kate's crying. I closed my eyes and drew in a deep breath, relegating myself to doing the one thing I knew wasn't smart right now.

I bypassed the idea of going to the gym and decided to knock on her door instead.

"Kate?" I asked.

I knocked softly, but all I heard was her voice. "What?"

I sighed. "Can I come in?"

She sniffled. "No. Go away."

But, my hand fell to the doorknob, and I opened the door.

"Of course, you'd come in anyway," Kate murmured.

I closed the door behind me and sat in a chair off to the side. "No wife of mine cries alone."

If looks could kill, I'd be six feet under. And when she went back to crying, I leaned forward.

"You can joke about it, or you can cry about it. But either way, know that I'll fix it, Kate."

She scoffed. "Whatever."

I wasn't sure whether it was the hangover that made me soft-hearted or the fact that I didn't like seeing anyone cry, but before I knew it, I was on the bed with her. I took her into my arms and let her head fall against my chest as she soaked my gym shirt with her tears. It killed me inside to feel her shaking violently with her sobs. The sadness pouring from her reminded me of my own, and I found myself blinking back tears I refused to shed any longer over the paths I had taken in my life. I had made my bed. I knew how to sleep in it. And as far as I was concerned, I had promises I needed to fulfill.

Which meant that a fake marriage didn't fit into any of my future plans.

"It's gonna be all right, I swear," I whispered.

Kate drew in broken breaths. "I–I–I–I–don't know how–how we—"

I ran my fingers through her hair. "Sh–sh–sh–sh–sh. You have to calm down for me a bit. I don't want you getting sick again."

She hicupped with her sobs. "I–I don't–I don't think—"

I wasn't sure what I thought would happen. Maybe I thought a kiss would snap Kate out of her crying trance and stop it altogether. Perhaps the crying was too intense, and I really was that uncomfortable with emotions. But, the next thing I knew, I gripped her hair and pulled her head back before planting my lips against hers.

And when the salty taint of her tears blazed a trail into her mouth, our tongues collided, rising up within me a need to have her.

Instead of pushing me away, like I figured she might, she draped her arms around my neck. She pulled me to the mattress, my body flush against hers as she quickly spread her legs. Apparently, she had the same idea, and I had no issues indulging in something to distract us both. I'd certainly make it worthwhile this time around.

With every touch of my lips against her skin, her crying turned to gasping. With every nip of my teeth against her pulse points, her gasping turned to moaning. Her tears dried up, giving way to the wetness between her legs that my tongue practically begged for, which only sank me between her thighs faster than I had anticipated.

I ripped her clothes off, hearing seams popping and stitches bursting as I clawed at her to get her naked. Her womanly scent wafted up to my nostrils, causing my cock to ache with need as it hung between my legs. I lapped up her slit, tasting her for the first time as her thighs quivered against my cheeks.

Then, she tangled her fingers into my hair and pulled me up her body.

"What?" I asked breathlessly.

She crashed our lips together. "Fill me up and take me away from this place."

Who was I to deny her what she wanted?

I slid off the bed and tugged off my clothes before reaching for her ankles. She squealed with delight as I pulled her to the edge of the mattress, tossing her calves over my shoulders. Her hands reached out for me, and I wrapped mine around her wrists, tugging her closer to me as my thickening girth fell against her drenched pussy lips.

I eased my cock into her tight, wet depths, watching her shiver as I bent her in half. And when I pinned her wrists above her head, her eyes bulged with pleasure.

"Oh, fuck," she groaned.

I pulled out and slammed back inside.

"Oh, yeah. Just like that." She whimpered. "More. Give me more, Boone."

Electricity sizzled through my veins as I pounded against her. I watched her glorious tits jump against her body as her nipples puckered into painful peaks. Her walls clamped down against me as she fell over the edge, shivering and jolting with her crushing orgasm.

But, I pulled out just before I exploded. Because I wasn't nearly done with her yet. "Over you go," I growled.

Her legs fell away from my shoulders, and I caught her ankles before they hit the floor. I flipped her over, bending her until her knees were perched against the edge of the bed. Kate panted for air as I held tightly against her hips, guiding my pulsing girth back into her swollen pussy.

"Oh, God," she groaned.

And with every pump of my hips against hers, I watched those toned little ass cheeks of hers tease me with their jiggling perfection.

"Goddammit, you're gorgeous," I grunted.

"Come for me," she said breathlessly, "I want to feel you let go."

I pulled her body back against my cock, fucking myself with her warmth. I gnashed my teeth together and let my inner beast take control as she called out my name into the heavens. The bed rocked so heavily that the frame began to scrape across the floor. I took steps as necessary, keeping my cock sheathed in her warmth as I approached my end. My balls pulled up. I felt my cock twitching against her walls. Her pussy collapsed around me as she choked on the letters of my name, trying so hard to call out to me.

I committed the sound to memory so I would never forget this moment.

And when my dick finally burst, I collapsed against her back.

With her stomach splayed against the bed and her legs

dangling off the sides, we both panted in tandem with one another. With every pump of my cock that shot threads of arousal deep within her body, I growled and fisted the comforter beneath her. I nuzzled my cheek against her warm skin and breathed her in as heavily as I could.

Then, the two of us climbed into her cock-eyed bed before she clamored back into my arms.

She panted softly against the crook of my neck as her naked body settled against my own. I looked up at the ceiling, trying to blink away the silver, star-like streaks that had bombarded my vision. Never in my life had I experienced an orgasm that powerful. Never had I enjoyed something so much with a woman that I wanted to go again. And again. Until she begged me to stop.

Then, her voice had to go and ruin it. "Boone?"

This isn't going to be good. "Yeah?"

She raised up, and I felt her eyes on the profile of my face. "Why couldn't you just tell me what the far-off look in your eye was about this morning."

I stiffened against her. "I don't know what you're talking about."

"You know," she said as she settled her chin against my chest, "when we were in the kitchen after we first woke up?"

I shrugged. "No clue. I was fine, though I'll admit I was also pretty angry."

"Boone, you're lying to me."

I slipped away from her. "I should go ahead and get dressed."

"I can't be with someone who can't be honest with me about the simplest of things."

I pulled my clothes back on. "Who said anything about us being together?"

The second the words flew out of my mouth, I wanted to take them back. The second I uttered that last little syllable, I knew I'd done irreparable damage. And when I turned around, gripping my shirt in my hands, I saw the walls come back up over Kate's eyes.

"Silly me," she said flatly.

I slid on my shirt quickly. "Kate, I didn't mean—"

She turned away from me. "You can close the door on your way out."

"Kate, just—"

"Thanks."

I looked over at the door and wondered if it was smart to leave. My fear, though, was that if I left, she'd think I was actually serious, and I'd never get another shot. Ever. My only option here was to be as open as I could without dredging up memories that had taken me months—even years—to properly bury.

So, I slipped back into bed with her beneath the covers— clothes and all—and let my arm slip around her waist.

"Kate," I said softly.

She sniffled. "I really hate you sometimes."

I nuzzled my nose against her bare shoulder. "You're right."

She paused. "What?"

I snickered. "I said, you're right. I was lying to you, and I shouldn't have."

It took a little while, but eventually, she rolled over and looked at me. "I guess empty apologies aren't as bad as no apology at all."

I sighed. "Look, it's just some really personal stuff back from my days in the military, and I don't like talking about it."

"Neither did my brother, but he knew it was for the best that he talk to someone."

"Yeah, I know."

She scooted a smidge closer to me. "Would you like to talk about it now? You know, open up like a regular person might to someone he likes?"

I shook my head slowly. "I'm pretty sure we're dealing with enough right now."

She rolled her eyes. "Then, seriously. Get the fuck out."

When she turned away from me, I didn't question what I needed to do. She needed to be alone, and I had a hell of a lot to think about. I slipped out of bed and padded over to her door, but not before stealing one last glance over my shoulder.

And when I heard Kate sigh, I decided to take her at face value.

At least I have work to keep me distracted from this shit.

Just like I felt distracted by the worries of my life whenever I was balls deep in Kate.

✣ 14 ✣

Kate

After lying around, feeling sorry for myself, I got up and slipped on the robe hanging on the hook behind the bathroom door. I bundled myself up, slipped into my house shoes, then stuck my cell phone into my pocket. I needed a change of scenery—something that didn't smell like the stench of regret and sorrow that hung around me in the air.

I also needed a place that didn't smell like Boone. With every whiff of his scent, I wanted him back against my body.

I forced myself out of my bedroom and walked toward the massive living room window walls. I pulled up a chair and sat right in front of them, gazing out over the city that had fucked over my life in less than twenty-four hours. I pulled my cell phone out and had the bright idea to call my manager, Marjorie. Maybe she knew a way out of the hole I had dug for myself, especially since she had helped me climb the ranks in the gym after quitting my teaching gig.

I dialed her number and held the phone to my ear, hoping and praying she'd pick up. It was a Saturday evening, so for all I knew, she'd be out and about with her husband. But, when she picked up, and I heard her sweet, comforting voice, I broke down crying.

"Whoa, whoa, whoa," she said. "Pump the brakes. What's going on?"

I drew in broken breaths. "Everything is ruined."

"Ruined, how? What's wrong? Do I need to come over?"

I shook my head. "Not. Home."

"Then where are you? I can come to get you."

My hiccuping sobs were back full force. "In. Vegas."

I cried over the phone to her without another word spoken. I cried so hard I thought I was going to vomit in my lap. The sun was just beginning to set, and it cast colors over the Vegas skyline that would have been beautiful on any other night, in any other scenario, with any other person.

But at that moment, it was yet another reminder of the beauty my life used to hold but didn't any longer.

"All right," Marjorie said after my crying calmed down, "start from the beginning. How did you get to Vegas?"

"Boone invited me, so I came along."

"Okay, we'll get into why you did that later. Where exactly in Vegas are you?"

I slouched into the chair. "It's the new resort in Vegas that opened up, what, last year?"

"Ah, okay. I know which one you're talking about."

I nodded slowly. "Yeah. I'm up in the penthouse."

"Penthouse is nice."

I drew in a stable breath before I closed my eyes. "I don't know what I'm going to do."

"I mean, I'm still stuck on the fact that you actually went anywhere with someone, much less that massive man with tattoos all over his torso."

I blinked. "Wait, what?"

"Yeah! Boone Remington, right? He came walking down the hallway, strutting his stuff one time, completely soaked like he took a damn shower with his clothes on."

A flush crept up my spine. "Really?"

"Yep. Peacocking the fuck out of his stance, too. He was wearing a white shirt, and it was plastered to him, and I noticed a bunch of tattoos beneath."

How the hell had I not noticed them when he was naked with me? "Do you know what kind of tattoos?"

She barked with laughter. "You're in Vegas with Boone Remington after making eyes at each other during your workout sessions, and you don't know the man's got tattoos? You're not doing Vegas right, girl."

No fucking joke. "What kinds of tattoos, Marjorie?"

"How the hell am I supposed to know?"

I closed my eyes. "Can you just—try to remember?"

She sighed. "Okay, okay. Uh... it looked like he was

covered in them. Lots of little ones, not like a cohesive design? If that makes sense?"

"Could you make out any of them? At all?"

She clicked her tongue. "A couple of them looked like emblems, maybe? Possibly slogans or sayings that mean something to him? How the hell should I know? The only man I stare down nowadays is my husband."

I pinched the bridge of my nose as everything slowly fell into place. "Shit."

"What?"

I sighed. "He was having flashbacks."

"Who? Boone?"

"Yes. I mean, no. I mean—fuck, I don't even know what I mean anymore."

For one, I felt like a slut. I'd slept with the man twice and had no idea he was clad in tattoos. But, another part of me was worried. If Boone had actually been having a flashback, I'd been too dumb and self-absorbed to notice. I mean, I knew what they looked like. I had helped Sebastian through them a lot, back when my brother was still alive. I should've been able to spot it.

The frozen body.

The far-off look.

The sweat permeating just above the brow.

I'm an idiot. "Marjorie?"

"Yeah?"

I licked my lips. "Can I call out for Monday as well? Or is that going to be an issue?"

She snickered. "I've been trying to tell you to take a damn vacation for as long as I can remember. You've been working straight-up hours since you quit your teaching job up at the high school, and I wouldn't blink an eye at giving you the entire week off if you wanted it."

I didn't hesitate. "Give me that. I'll cover shifts for people next weekend if necessary, but I'll need this upcoming week off."

"Great. Finally, you talk some sense."

I smiled softly. "Thanks."

"Hey, don't thank me. I'm just doing my job."

I quirked an eyebrow. "It's your job to listen to your employs cry over the phone and go on about shit you don't understand?"

"No, that's my job at work. But this is my job as a friend."

My heart warmed so quickly it brought tears back to my eyes. "Nice to know I have one."

She clicked away on a keyboard before she stopped. "Got your shifts covered. We'll see you next Saturday, okay?"

I stood to my feet. "I really appreciate this, thank you."

"And if you need anything between now and then, don't hesitate to call. Got it?"

I turned toward the hallway. "Got it."

"Let me know when you get back into town so I know you're home safe."

I started my way toward Boone's bedroom. "I can do that, yeah."

"Good. We'll talk soon."

"Talk soon. Bye."

"Bye."

I hung up and slid the phone into my pocket. I eased myself down the hallway, making my way toward Boone's makeshift office. I heard him typing away furiously, and I eased the door open, finding him hunched over at his desk.

And when I closed the door behind me, he didn't let up. "More screen-flashing emergencies?"

He didn't even flinch. "Nothing so far."

I leaned against the door. "So, question."

"Answer."

"Where is this conference you're supposed to be attending today?"

That's when his typing stopped. It stopped, and it left an eerie blanket of silence that stilled my restless soul.

"Boone?"

He spun around in his chair. "Kate."

I slid my hands into the pockets of the robe. "There's no conference, is there?"

He stood to his feet. "No, there isn't."

I resisted the urge to be upset with him. "Why would you lie about something like that?"

He cleared his throat, searching for the words. "Honestly?"

"It would be a nice change for once."

He sighed. "I deserved that."

I pushed myself away from the door and took a step toward him. "So? You gonna spill?"

He chuckled awkwardly, and for the life of me, it was a first. I'd never seen *the* Boone Remington feeling awkward when doing anything. But, as he slid his hands into his short gym pockets and looked around the room to search for more words to use, I felt a grin sliding across my face.

For once, Boone was vulnerable.

And it was a good look on him.

"Honestly, Kate, I never thought you'd actually go away with me for any other reason other than you being with me to help me out with something."

I nodded slowly. "You figured if you asked for a weekend alone that I'd say no?"

"And I admit, it is my MO, but it's not because I wanted to embarrass you or corner you or any of that stupid bullshit I did as a kid. I simply wanted to spend time with you, so I came up with a reason that I knew had the best chance of working."

I furrowed my brow. "So, you wanted to go away with me somewhere all this time?"

He shrugged. "Yeah?"

I scoffed. "Why?"

His eyes finally met mine. "What?"

I shook my head. "I don't get it. After all we've done to one another and how we've made each other feel, why the hell would you ever want to be anywhere with me?"

And he didn't miss a beat. "Maybe you don't get how amazing you are, so I wanted a chance to prove to you just how wrong you are."

Maybe I've been all wrong about him from the start. "Boone?"

He held his head high with pride. "I can take whatever it is you have to say."

I smirked as I walked toward him, my neck craned back to keep his gorgeous eyes in view. "Would you like to have dinner with me tonight?"

It took him a second to respond. But when he did, that cheeky little grin of his spread across his face, and his chuckle filled my soul with delight. "Only if I can take you out on a true, bonafide date."

I pressed my finger against his chest. "It's a date, then."

And before either of us could ruin the moment with our pesky emotions that we didn't enjoy indulging, I spun around in my house shoes and made my way for the door. I didn't want anything to ruin this moment. I didn't want to give one of us the opportunity to say something neither of us could take back. So, with my hands in my robe pockets and my spine straight, I made my way for my bedroom while planning what outfit—and lingerie set—I wanted to wear out tonight in my head.

❧ 15 ❧

Boone

With my best suit on and my coat buttoned only once around my waist, I rapped my knuckles softly against Kate's bedroom door. I had to pull some strings in order to get us a last-minute reservation at one of the hottest French bistros Vegas had to offer, but I knew it would be worth it.

The second Kate opened the door, though, I didn't give a shit about the food.

"This look okay?" she asked.

My jaw slowly dropped open as she held her arms out and gave me a little twirl. And I swear to fuck on high, I could have shoved her into that room and made her my meal as well as my dessert for the night. Her chocolate-colored dress clung tightly to her curves, accenting the toned definition of her muscles she clearly took pride in. The barely there outline of panties and a bra made me wonder what racy little number she had on beneath everything, and her sparkling jewelry was offset by her matching velvet stilettos.

"Jesus," I said breathlessly, "I think it'll be the first night people don't stare at me for once."

She giggled and swatted my chest playfully, but I was serious. The muted colors of her outfit brought out the strawberry-blonde notes of her hair and accented the way her dark-green eyes glistened with mischievous delight. She had her hair pulled back into a half-ponytail that was wispily curled and fluffed to create a volume of softness I wanted to sink my hands into...while she was sucking on my cock.

"Ready to head out?" she asked.

I watched her clasp a matching clutch between her arm and her side, and I never knew I could be so jealous about an inanimate object.

"Ready when you are," I said as I held out my hand.

She let me settle my palm against the small of her back, and it was all I could do to keep my dick in line. I led her down to a convertible I had rented for us and opened her door to let her in. I jogged around to my side and hopped in without opening the door, causing Kate to fall apart in a fit of giggles that seduced my ear into a puddle of goop.

And as we made our way to the bistro, Kate let my hand sit softly against her bare knee.

When we got to the bistro, I offered her my arm. I

ushered her inside before we were led down into a private
room in the restaurant's cellar where soft music played amid
dimly lit lights. It was a far cry away from the hustle and
bustle of the streets above us. In fact, it almost felt as if we
weren't anywhere near Vegas any longer.

I pulled out Kate's chair and offered my hand for her to
sit. But when I took up my position in front of her, I saw her
eyes lingering up and down my form.

"To what do I owe the pleasure of your gaze?" I asked.

She shook her head. "I don't want to ruin the date just yet.
This is too perfect."

I crossed my leg over my knee. "You couldn't ruin it."

She grinned. "That a challenge?"

I chuckled. "If you want it to be, sure."

Our waiter interrupted us. "My apologies for the intrusion, but I have a bottle of wine for the both of you that I
believe will go splendidly with your meals this evening."

Kate's eyebrows rose. "Did you order ahead of time?"

My grin grew devious. "How does *beouf bourguignon, blan-
quette de veau, soupe a L'oignon, bouillabaisse, fondue savoyarde*, and
tarte tatin sound?"

"Uh... sounds good?"

I nodded. "Wonderful. Then, yes. I ordered ahead of
time."

She giggled. "You're something else, you know that?"

I motioned to the waiter. "Feel free to pour whenever
you're ready, and leave the bottle, please."

The waiter nodded. "Of course, sir."

The rich and tantalizing aroma of the wine made my mouth water, but I reached for my glass of water instead. I didn't want to gorge myself on alcohol the way I had the other night. I actually wanted to enjoy my evening with Kate, not simply because of the sex I wanted to come after all of this. I wanted to enjoy my evening because I wanted to create positive memories with a lovely woman who never once left the back of my mind after all these years.

"To us," Kate said as she held up her glass.

I picked up my wine glass and followed suit. "To us, to now, and to the future."

She smiled. "Here, here."

We clinked our glasses, and I sipped the wine, and dammit, if it wasn't so good that I actually groaned. Kate started giggling, and I set down my glass, grinning at her as I dabbed at my lips.

"Sorry, that was just amazing," I murmured.

She tipped her entire glass back before refilling it. "Trust me, I know."

"Be careful, or we'll end up like we were last night again."

She shrugged. "I mean, we already got married. What else can we do to make the weekend exciting?"

I leaned forward. "If you say, 'get pregnant,' I'm going to get up and walk out."

She barked with laughter. "Yeah, no thanks. Maybe in the distant future, when I'm not so paranoid about the people I love dying in droves. But, not now, and certainly not in the *near* future."

"You have that same fear, too?"

Her eyes slowly met mine as she set down the wine bottle. "You know, that wet shirt of yours when we hooked up in the shower at the gym exposed some of your tattoos."

I leaned back. "Dodging the question, I see."

She shrugged. "If you answer honestly, then I will. But seeing as you're the one with truth issues, you'll have to go first."

"So you know you can trust me with what you tell me, right?"

She nodded. "Among other things."

I licked my lips. "Okay, yes. I do have tattoos. Though, it tickles me to know that you didn't see them earlier."

She rolled her eyes playfully. "I was a bit preoccupied with other things."

I winked at her. "Good to know I can distract so beautifully."

She blushed, and the color looked fantastic on her. "So, tattoos. What are they about?"

I reached for my water glass. "You know, from my time in the military. Some slogans I take to heart. Things like that."

"Any dates?"

My stare grew firm. "That's a pretty pointed and specific question."

She sighed. "My brother had a couple of dates tattooed onto him as well. You know, during his time in the military. I'm wondering if your dates are for the same purpose as his."

I sipped my water and placed it back onto the table. "The

dates are from special moments in the service that I never want to forget."

"And thank you for it."

"For what?"

"For your service."

I shook my head curtly. "I hate it when people say that."

She shrugged. "Then, I won't say it again. But, I still mean it."

Our fondue appetizer came out, but neither of us quit staring at each other. Even as the waiter topped off our wine glasses and walked away, neither of our gazes wobbled. So, I decided to keep playing twenty questions with this gorgeous woman to see just how much I could push before I ruined everything—like I always did.

"Why did you come here with me?" I asked.

Kate's face grew sheepish. "What?"

I settled my hands into my lap. "Why did you agree to come here with me? You said it yourself, coming here with each other after our past and our current history was a bit provocative, to say the least. So, why agree to it?"

Her gaze fell to her lap. "Honestly?"

"I'd like that, yes."

She sighed heavily. "The original plan was to come here with you to try to get you back for how much hurt you caused me as a teenager."

"And the new plan?"

Her eyes slowly rose to meet my own. "To try to salvage

the ashes of my life after losing the only person who ever gave a shit about me."

Her words hung heavily in my mind before I drew in a deep breath. "What did your brother do in the military?"

Her eyes watered over. "You really want to do this now? I figured this was at least a two-bottles-of-wine conversation."

"It's your decision, but I'm open to listening to whatever you want to tell me."

"You know it goes both ways with me, right?"

I smiled softly. "I know."

She smiled in kind, too. "Good. Just making sure."

"So, what did he do? What was his job?"

She drew in a deep breath through her nose. "Uh, he was infantry in the army. He enlisted essentially after he graduated high school."

"Wanted to shoot at the bad guys?"

She snickered. "Yeah, like an idiot."

I blinked. "Did Sebastian travel a lot?"

She nodded mindlessly. "He loved that part. Going to new places. Experiencing new things. Meeting people and helping people. He really believed in all of that shit, you know?"

I chuckled bitterly. "Yeah, I know."

She swallowed hard. "Then, three years ago, he just died. He was deployed, and I had talked to him a couple of days before he went out on patrol. The next thing I knew, I was coming home from teaching bratty little high school kids all day, and two military men were standing on my doorstep."

"Jesus," I whispered.

She wiped at her tears. "After that, everywhere I went, there he was. In school. In my classroom. In the faces of my students. Everywhere I looked, there were memories of Sebastian and me, just roaming the halls of our high school with no cares in the world."

"I'm so sorry, Kate."

"And you know what? That's exactly why I quit my job. That's exactly why I took a job with the gym, too. Sebastian hated gyms. He said he never wanted to pay for something he could get outside and make up himself. I knew it was the one place in fucking Conroe, Texas, where I could get away from his memory."

"I know how that feels."

Her eyes grew angry as her memories ripped her back. "And you know what else? Maybe I came to Vegas with you because I can't afford a vacation on my salary at the gym. Maybe I wanted a weekend to get away from all this fucking pain I've held inside for the past three years. Just for a couple of days, you know? But maybe because I always need a bull-shit excuse to do something good for me, I needed to convince myself that it was okay to go and live my life for a little bit despite the fact that my brother can't."

God, if she only knew how similar we really were. "Has the weekend helped at all?"

She laughed before a tear streaked her cheek. "Yeah, not really."

"I suppose that was a dumb question, yeah."

Silence fell between us before I leaned forward, planting

my forearms against the table. "Let me venture a wild guess about something."

She sighed as her gaze fell back into her lap. "Sure, go ahead."

"I take it that talking helps you out in these kinds of scenarios? Which is why you're trying to get me to talk?"

And to my shock, she shook her head. "No."

I blinked. "No?"

Her head rose up until our eyes met. "Talking only hurts. But, working out helps. Hence how I climbed the ladder of the gym so quickly."

Then, I finally reached for a fondue spear for my food. "So, you said something about being a teacher beforehand?"

She reached for one as well. "Yeah. I taught high school English at the school where we graduated."

"Wow. That's a serious accomplishment."

"I loved it, too. Despite how bratty those kids can sometimes be, I loved going to work there. It reminded me of so many good times. So many good memories."

"Even with everything I did?"

She giggled softly. "You weren't my entire high school career. Just a rough part of it."

I furrowed my brow. "I really am sorry, Kate. For everything."

She nodded softly, her eyes dancing between my own. "I know you are. I believe you."

Relief flooded my veins. "Good. I'm glad."

I loved finding out all of these things about her. Yet, I

hated that I didn't have the balls to offer up any information about myself without getting pissed off or tired or fucking sad.

"You know, I started out at the front desk in the gym," she said.

I dipped my bread into the cheese fondue. "Did you enjoy the cushy desk job?"

She dipped a piece of meat into the cheese. "I wouldn't call it 'cushy,' but it was nice for a depressed, pissed off girl who wanted to lash out at the world. It didn't take me long after that to get the certifications I needed to become a professional trainer so I could run classes and take clients. Then, Marjorie—that's my boss-slash-friend—moved me into a full-time position doing nothing but taking clients and running lunch-time classes."

"You should be very proud of yourself. It's hard for some people to pivot on the spot like that."

She shrugged. "I guess my depression left me with no choice. It was either take a new job or find a way out."

Then, after she slid the piece of cheese-covered meat off the end of her spear, she chewed and leaned forward before she swallowed, commanding my attention as her voice lowered steadily.

"But, the reason working out helped me is because I told the weights my secrets, Boone. I talked to them, just like I would have talked to an actual person."

I paused. "Why?"

She leaned back up. "Because I knew those weights

wouldn't judge me, nor would they tell a soul what I said to them. I told those weights some of my deepest, darkest secrets, and that's why they made me feel better."

"Maybe I should try that sometime," I murmured.

She didn't skip a beat, either. "Just know, Remington, that I'll be your weights. If and when you're ever ready to talk about what it is you carry so deep down inside, I'll listen without judgment, and my lips will never utter anything you tell me to anyone else. You have my word."

And before I knew it, the sincerity in her eyes and the tone of her voice left me doing only one thing—taking in a deep, even breath before my lips started moving.

16

Kate

When I watched Boone draw in a deep breath, I readied myself for whatever snarky remarks he had to dish up this time around. But, I was pleasantly surprised at what he said when he started talking. So surprised, in fact, that I forgot all about the food growing cold in front of us.

"You know, Sebastian and I have that in common. I essentially enlisted right after high school. The Marines had this little booth set up at some career field whatever day the school had for the seniors, and it resonated with me. I mean, a full-time paycheck while shooting up bad guys and no school? Sign me the fuck up, you know?"

I nodded, but I didn't say anything. I didn't want to do

anything to jeopardize his state of mind. Because apparently, he was in a sharing mood for once.

"I always hated school, too," he continued. "All I wanted was to compete in the rodeo, lift weights, and hang out with my friends. Which I figured was what the military would be all about. I mean, I had buddies who enlisted, and they talked about all this damn downtime they had, and all the long weekends, and mandatory holidays off. Shit like that. It sounded like a damn dream."

I smiled softly. "I bet so."

He leaned back in his seat, looking almost defeated. "I saw myself traveling all over the world. Going and seeing all of these exotic places and meeting all of these unusual people. Some of the guys and myself, while we were in basic, made a pledge to one another that for every country we visited, we'd screw at least one hot-ass girl and come home to tell the tale."

I snickered. "Sounds like eighteen-year-olds to me."

His eyes looked off into the distance. "It never once occurred to me that the promises we made to one another would be the exact reason we scrambled to get home after those dusty, dingy, disgusting deployments."

My heart broke for him. "I'm sure."

He chewed on the inside of his cheek. "And I visited a lot of places, too. My favorite was Italy. It's the only country I visited for any sort of temporary duty deployment that I actually want to go back and enjoy as a civilian. I mean, the food is top fucking notch, and there's no better wine on this planet."

The thought made me smile, but I tried to keep it buried

because something in my gut told me this wasn't going to be a conversation worth the grins I felt as he talked about what he liked about certain countries.

Then, we crash-landed into the real issue. "Did Sebastian ever talk about *that* deployment?"

I blinked. "Come again?"

"You know, the deployment that always changes a military person? Did he ever talk about it?"

I knew exactly what he was talking about. "Sometimes I could get him to talk, yeah."

He scoffed and looked off to the side. "Every military personnel has one. That one deployment that changes the way they view the world forever."

"What happened on yours? Or do you not want to talk about it?"

His gaze slowly came back to mine, and I figured he'd tell me to fuck off. But instead, he drew in another deep breath and started talking. So, I strapped myself in for the ride.

"I was tasked with spending fifteen months in Kabul. We were essentially going to switch out individuals who had been there for almost two damn years, and I was ready for it. DeShawn and me against the world. That's how we saw it."

I giggled quietly. "Sebastian knew a DeShawn. But, his buddy from basic was a man by the name of Lucas."

If what I said registered with Boone, he didn't acknowledge it. "DeShawn and I were ready to tackle the world. Ready to bring a little pep into everyone's step for the next fifteen fucking months. And everything was going according to plan. Everything was running like clockwork until a last-minute patrol we were scheduled to be on departed from the base."

I felt my gut clenching as tears rose in Boone's eyes.

"DeShawn, me, and two other guys piled into this idiotic Humvee and were bee-bopping around like we owned the damn place. We high-fived the locals and stopped to play with some kids who were kicking a ball around. We even used some of our own money to buy snacks for everyone playing and working up a sweat outside. It was the best fucking moment of that deployment. And then, we started making our way back."

I swallowed hard. "You were ambushed."

He blinked his tears away again as his voice fell flat. "Before I could blink, the blast had the Humvee on its side. One of the guys didn't even make it out of the goddamn Humvee after we hit that damn IED. The three of us who were left clawed our way out, and that's when bullets started flying. And the other guy—Branson—was struggling to get his basic buddy—Carl—out of the back seat."

"Jesus," I whispered.

He swallowed hard. "We scurried for cover and started firing, but bullets were flying in all sorts of fucking directions. I radioed for help as much as I could before a bullet grazed my shoulder and sliced the wire that connected me to the damn thing in the first place. It was the biggest fucking shit-show I'd ever seen in my damn life, and we knew that—even on a good note—help was still at least ten minutes out. And I knew we didn't have enough ammo on us for even five minutes of the shit we dealt with."

I swallowed hard. "That's—my God, Boone."

He closed his eyes. "DeShawn was hellbent on not leaving Branson and Carl's bodies behind, but I had to hold him back in the trench we jumped into. I couldn't bear to lose him, you know? We'd been together essentially our entire career, and I wasn't letting him go out like that. But, DeShawn kept yelling about taking their bodies home and keeping them intact. And before I knew it, he slipped out of my grasp."

My lower lip quivered. "I'm so sorry, Boone."

His eyes opened, and I found nothing but dark ice in his stare. "I heard him gurgling on his own blood when he was shot. Anger welled within me unlike anything I'd ever experienced, and I blacked out. I don't remember anything at all until I was staring down at DeShawn's almost-lifeless eyes, begging him to say something. Anything. And when he found the strength to speak, he made me make a promise."

I was almost scared to ask. "What was the promise?"

His gaze fell to his lap. "He made me promise that I'd find a good life outside of the military and that I'd find myself a good woman like the one he left behind after tucking tail and running from his hometown."

Tears streaked my face as Boone snickered.

"Guess he and I had more in common than I wanted to admit back in those days."

There was so much familiarity in his story versus Sebastian's. And when Boone focused back on me, his eyes were glassy with tears he refused to shed. Mine dripped down my face as I studied him. Studied the pain etched into the wrinkles in his forehead and the ache slathered across his gaze. I wanted nothing more than to take him into my arms.

"They gave me a medal for that, you know," he said heatedly.

I cocked my head. "For what?"

He sniffled and wiped at his eyes. "For staying with my men. For slaughtering the terrorists who had been shooting at us. I don't remember shit, but everyone convinced me that I had single-handedly taken out the nine men gunning us down while DeShawn lay there in my lap. And they gave me a fucking medal for it. For killing nine different people and losing three of my men, Kate. They rewarded me for that shit. They gave me a goddamn medal for killing and losing. I mean, who the fuck does that?"

The second the tears rip-roared down his face, I shot up from my chair. He bowed his head and sniffled deeply as I slid myself into his lap. I wrapped my arms around his neck as he settled his forehead against my shoulder. The muted sounds of his crying shattered my heart into pieces.

"It's okay," I said through my own tears, "I've got you, Boone. You're safe now. It's going to be okay."

He wrapped his arms tightly around me. "I lost them, Kate. I lost all of them."

I kissed the top of his head. "I've got you. It's going to be okay, I swear. I'll find a way to make it okay."

He shook his head. "It's never going to be okay. Never. Holy fuck, what the hell have I done?"

And as his body trembled against mine, fraught with tears that were probably unshed after all these years, I closed my eyes and steadied myself, becoming the rock Boone needed as he fell weak against my body.

❧ 17 ❧

Boone

My brother's voices kept flying over my head as I sat in the meeting. It felt like ages since Kate and I had flown back from Vegas, and I longed for our little bubble of solitude again. Our last evening in Vegas after our particularly volatile dinner was filled with tears, laughter, and cuddling.

Just—just cuddling.

We stayed up all night until we had to leave to catch our plane. And what did we do that entire time? We talked. All we did was talk. We talked about high school, and I got to hear her perspective of what I had done and how it had made her feel. I got the chance to apologize for things that had completely slipped my mind... as well as a few things I knew I would never forget. For the first time in my life, I got to break down without being judged, without being told to suck it up because I was a soldier, without being told that I needed to "get used to it;" otherwise, I didn't need to re-enlist.

All I wanted was to go back to that night and keep reliving it.

It was a first for me in many regards. It was the first time I'd never tried to sleep with a woman after our first date. It was the first time I'd been so physically close to a woman without ripping her clothes to shreds. It was also the first time I felt comfortable enough to cry, knowing the person I was crying to wouldn't get up and walk away. I found myself wondering if it would ever happen again.

"Boone?"

Bryce's voice caught my ear, and my eyes whipped toward him. "Yep?"

"You, uh, got any input on this conversation?"

All five of my other brothers were staring at me while that tinfoil wedding ring burned a hole in my pocket. Why the hell had I brought it to work with me in the first place? I had no clue. But, one minute, I was rushing out the door for work, and the next, I was ripping that damned thing off my finger before anyone saw me wearing it. And now, I prayed my brothers didn't see the circular bulge against my outer thigh.

"I know what he's thinking about," Wyatt said with a grin.

I clicked my tongue. "He's right. I *am* thinking about how the hell we're going to approach Mr. Blanchard with this. Because at this point, it's our only course of action."

My brothers launched into another conversation while Wyatt simply stared at me. But, I didn't give him the satisfaction of one-upping me in the middle of a business meeting. We were getting strange-enough looks as it was, with people passing by the conference room and trying to act like they weren't peeking in at the six of us. Rarely did we all gather in the same spot unless it was an emergency. At this point, the entire company knew we were flying our flags at half-mast.

"I still think we should go straight to the police," Ryan said.

Bryce shook his head. "I'm in favor of the quiet approach. Give him a chance to explain himself. Because I really don't think Mr. Blanchard is behind all of this."

I scoffed. "Trust me, no one thinks he is. But, I get where Ryan and Will are coming from. If we go up to him and show him what we know, and he does know something? He's liable to start covering shit up before we can point the police in his direction."

Will pointed at me. "Exactly. That is why I really believe we should just pass this information on to the cops like we have in the past and be done with this already. Boone, you ready to start upping our security?"

I shrugged. "Hell, you guys authorize the transactions, and I'll get everything switched over to more secure servers that not even hackers in the CIA could crack."

Bart furrowed his brow. "Wait, you can really do that?"

I chuckled. "It's expensive as fuck, but I'm not taking chances right now. In both instances, whoever this is, tore through a fucking security system I built myself without batting a damn eyelash. We're dealing with someone who's got some serious experience."

Will sighed. "Or, the money to hire someone with some serious experience."

Ryan pointed at Will. "That sounds more like Mr. Blanchard."

Will held out his arms. "And if we tell him what we know, he'll start burning his paper trail before the police can even get to his fucking place."

Eventually, we all ended up taking a vote and taking the private way out, voting four to two. So, we all swiveled in our chairs and pulled the blackout shades while I got the video conference up and running with Mr. Blanchard. Thank fuck, the conference room was sound-proofed.

And after a few rings, he picked up. "Listen, Boone, I'm in a bit of a—oh, hello."

Bryce stood and clasped his hands behind his back. "Mr. Blanchard! Thank you for speaking with us on such short notice."

He swiveled to face the screen. "To what do I owe the pleasure of all six of you?"

Bryce didn't miss a beat. "We simply wanted to ask you a few questions. That's all."

He nodded. "All right, but make it quick. My daughter's coming over in a little bit with my grandbaby, and I'd like to have lunch with them on time."

Wyatt took the reins as he stood. "It won't take very long, Mr. Blanchard. You have our word."

He nodded. "Very well. What's on your minds, boys?"

Wyatt's eye twitched. "There have been a couple of disconcerting events that have happened over the course of the past couple of weeks."

"Oh? How so?"

I leaned back and analyzed his every move. His every word. His every fucking facial expression as he responded and reacted to Wyatt. Hell, I even broke down the tone of his voice just for shits and giggles. I did a lot of that back in the military just to stay alive some days, and I learned that reading someone usually ended up saving me a great deal of heartache in the end.

People lied a lot, and it was astounding how many more people lied right to others' faces.

Mr. Blanchard cleared his throat. "Any reason you boys are dancing around what you really want to ask?"

Wyatt snickered. "Then, I suppose I'll get to the point."

He looked back at all of us before he eyed me, and I nodded. I was ready for his reaction. I'd gotten a baseline of what he looked like when telling the truth, courtesy of Wyatt's nonchalant questions. And I was ready to sink this fucker into the ground.

"Mr. Blanchard," Wyatt said as he turned back to the screen, "over the past little while, we've had two significant attacks on our security systems. One was an individual hack that searched around in our databanks for a while until Boone could corner it, and the second one was a virus that sank itself into our systems to root for something specific. It came from a piece of spam mail one of our part-time employees in PR opened by accident."

Mr. Blanchard blinked. "And?"

"And, when Boone back-traced the IP address on both attacks, the IP address registered itself with your computer."

He paused. "I'm sorry, what?"

Wyatt nodded. "Your computer. Whoever enacted both of the hacks did so from the home office you're currently sitting in—with the computer you're currently staring at. You wouldn't happen to know anything about that, would you?"

I watched Mr. Blanchard's face grow pale, and I knew we had him. So, I didn't wait for Wyatt to start in on the questions again.

I simply stood and did it myself. "If you know something, Mr. Blanchard—because we all believe you're not the person who did any of this—it's going to be better if you work with us."

Bryce jumped in. "He's right. All we want are answers. We aren't looking to press charges and ruin someone's life."

Bart stepped up to the plate. "We run a smooth operation, but we don't run like other businesses. If someone is looking for something because they need help or a leg-up on the competition or whatever, we're more than willing to sit down and share what we know."

Mr. Blanchard finally cleared his throat. "That isn't possible. There are very few people who have access to my home office."

My head tilted off to the side. "Who has access, sir?"

He sighed. "Only my daughter and me. And since my daughter has access, my grandson is usually in here with her."

Wyatt chuckled. "Well, rest assured that your grandson is cleared as a suspect."

"Wyatt," Bryce hissed.

But, I saw how red Mr. Blanchard's face started to turn. "My daughter has nothing to do with whatever it is you're insinuating happened. Are you sure it wasn't user error on your end?"

I chuckled. "I've worked in cybersecurity for the military, Mr. Blanchard. I built our security system. I don't make mistakes."

"Yeah, well, man isn't infallible, and that includes you, Boone. Where the hell do you get off accusing my daughter—"

Wyatt held his hands up. "We aren't accusing anyone of anything. All we want are answers."

Ryan stepped in and tried to calm down the tense situation. "Is there any way we could speak with your daughter? Just to get her to take on things?"

Mr. Blanchard's face grew cold. "Not unless you guys have a warrant."

I sighed. "Remember what's at stake here, sir. It's not just our company on the line. It's your place on our board of investors. Something like this would be in distinct violation of the contract you signed with us, and we don't want to have to do something like that simply because you think you're protecting someone. We aren't here to prosecute. We want to settle this quietly. But, we need your cooperation if we're going to do that."

Wyatt shrugged. "But, if we have to chase things down, we will. Or, the police can."

"Will you shut up?" Bryce hissed.

Mr. Blanchard scoffed. "Well, when you have your warrant, let me know. But until then? Don't you dare call last minute unless it's for business."

Wyatt held out his arms. "And what would you call this?"

I pinched the bridge of my nose as Mr. Blanchard hung up our phone call. I heard my brothers cursing Wyatt beneath their breath, but I wanted to wrap my hand around his throat. We had him. I had him. We had him in the perfect spot, and Wyatt's mouth fucking blew it.

Just like it always did.

"Are you serious?" Ryan asked as he turned to Wyatt.

Wyatt shrugged. "He's guilty as sin. Ask Boone."

Everyone turned to me, and I cracked my neck. "He's hiding something. But, he wasn't lying with any of the answers he gave us."

Bart nodded. "Either that or at least he believes he isn't lying."

"So, we have nothing," Will said.

The room fell silent before I clicked my tongue. "What now?"

We all looked around the room at each other before all eyes were on Bryce. He'd been the head of this company ever since Dad had stepped down and retired. Which meant that he needed to give the okay.

And when Bryce nodded his head, Ryan pulled out his phone. "I'll let the police know."

Will raked his hands through his hair. "I'll stick around until they show up. Boone?"

I thumbed over my shoulder. "Everything's in a red folder on top of my desk. Just hand it to the police. I got a few things that need to be signed off on before I can join you for the fiasco."

Ryan hung up the phone and came back inside. "The lead investigator on our case is on the way with a couple of his guys. They'd like to take a look at our security cameras and footage of the hacking? Is that even possible?"

I nodded. "Show them to my office. There's a file folder on my computer entitled 'Hacking Events.' It's right there on the home screen. Open it up. There are two videos. I screen-recorded both incidents."

Bart patted my shoulder. "This is why we pay you the big bucks, dude."

I chuckled wryly. "Yeah, well, I'd gladly give up half that salary not to have to deal with Mr. Blanchard's shit."

And for the first time all day, my brothers and I shared a moment of laughter together.

Making it feel like, for a second, that everything might turn out all right.

18

Kate

"One, hoo, two, hoo, three, hoo, four, hoo, five, hoo, six!" I set down the weights and shook out my arms before picking them up again. "One, hoo! Two, hoo! Three, hoo! Four, hoo! Five, hoo! Six!" I dropped the weights that time and drew in deep breaths before I lifted them one last time. "One! Hoo! Two! Hoo! Three! Hoo! Four! Hoo! Five! Hoo! Six!" And when I finally dropped the weights, I collapsed onto the mat and reached for my water bottle.

I stretched out my legs and lifted my hands above my head. With my water bottle off to the side, I leaned forward, stretching out my lower back and hamstrings as I controlled my breathing. Sweat poured down my body, drenching the mat beneath me as my legging and sports bra clung to me in a fit of soaked ecstasy. And with every movement I made, I felt that damn piece of shit wedding ring bouncing around in my bra against my tits.

Why the hell I'd forgotten to take that thing off, I'd never know. One second, I was marching out of the house to get in a nice workout while on my week-long break, and the next second, I had to duck into a dark corner and pull the damn thing off my finger.

I felt confused and conflicted. I felt off-kilter and not quite there. The absence of Boone after spending an entire weekend with him hit harder than I wanted to admit, and I wasn't sure what to do with that piece of information. Did I miss him? Yeah. I mean, the last part of our little weekend getaway was actually kind of nice. After dinner, we went back to the penthouse, changed into some more comfortable clothes, poured ourselves another glass of wine, and simply talked.

We watched the twinkling stars over the skyline of Vegas and talked.

We turned the television on and aimlessly watched it while we talked.

We even cuddled up on the couch with one too many glasses of wine in our system and stumbled around with our words to keep talking.

We talked so much that we didn't once go to sleep. And by the time we got on our first-class flight home, we slept so hard that neither of us budged until the stewardess softly shook both of us awake.

"All right," I groaned as I got off the floor, "time to do some clean-and-jerks."

After setting myself up with the weights, I checked my form in the mirror before reaching for the bar. I eased it up, rolling my shoulders back before I thrust my hips forward and brought the bar up to rest just against my chin. My arms hoisted the bar into the air, straightening but not locking out. And after bringing the bar back down in another smooth motion, I set it down before going a second time.

And a third time.

And a fourth time.

I lost myself in the rhythmic concoction of the exercise. That was the thing I loved the most about weights. Someone could do the same thing over and over and get new results every single time. Physics in the gym seemed to go against every law of social humanity out there, yet it worked to our benefit.

But, by the time my arms gave out, my feet were slippery from the amount of sweat I was stepping on.

I picked up my water bottle and lifted it up, expanding my lungs to take one more massive breath of air before I squirted the room temperature water into my mouth. I felt droplets trickling down my neck, finding their death between my tits. I felt that stupid ring pressing against my skin. I felt the burning sensation of emptiness against my finger.

However, before I could put my water bottle down and go for one last round to do me in for the day, Boone chuckled behind me.

"I get why they put that shot in the movies now."

I caught his stare in the reflection of the wall-to-wall mirrors in front of me. He walked up and started rubbing my back, and the sensation caused my eyes to flutter closed. The moment was short-lived, though, because less than a second later, he pulled his hand away and looked down at his palm.

"You're soaked in sweat, Kate."

I shrugged. "How'd you find me?"

Boone wiped his hand off on his jeans. "Well, I went to your house, and you weren't there, so I figured this was the most likely place to try next."

I nodded, but I didn't say anything. I was all out of words to use.

However, Boone stepped up beside me and gazed down at the top of my head. "Want to talk about it?"

I simply shrugged.

So, Boone pressed on. "I thought we got past this bullshit yesterday."

I sighed. "I know, I know. Old dogs and all that."

He grinned. "You're hardly old. Or a dog."

"That's your label, right?" I chuckled.

He quirked an eyebrow. "Old? Or a dog?"

I finally looked up at him. "Why not both?"

"Oh, the words. They wound. They wound so deeply." He clenched his heart.

I giggled before I cleared my throat and took another pull of my water. "I had a nightmare about Sebastian when I lay down to take a nap this afternoon, and I haven't been able to shake it. That's all."

Boone wrapped his arms around me, pulling me in for a tight hug. "Come here, beautiful."

I was shocked that he even considered hugging me, seeing as how I was so damn sweaty. But, his arms were so comforting, and hearing him call me such a wonderful pet name made my heart melt. And as I wrapped my arms around his strong form, I drew in his scent deeply through my nose, finding that it relaxed me more than it should have.

"It's okay to let it out, you know," Boone murmured.

I sniffled. "I hate crying in public."

He squeezed me tighter. "No one has to know if they can't see you." As he shuffled us over into a dark corner, I started crying against his chest.

I cried so hard that he sat down and pulled me into his lap. I cried so hard that I got snot on his shirt. I mean, fucking hell, I cried so hard that I couldn't catch my breath, and it felt like I'd run a damn marathon after all the weight-lifting I'd done.

"I miss him so much," I choked out.

Boone kissed my temple. "I know. Trust me, I get it."

"I'm so–so sorry you–you do."

He nuzzled his nose against my skin. "I'm right here. I'm not going anywhere. Okay?"

I clung to him as tightly as possible until my tears finally dried up. And when they did, I drew in a deep breath as I sat up. Boone's wondrous brown eyes laced with amber specks twinkled as he smiled at me, and dammit if the thing wasn't as contagious as it looked. I found myself smiling with him as my tears dried up, and the residual dwellings of the nightmare slowly faded away.

I wiped my sweat off the tip of his nose. "Sorry for getting you all sweaty."

Boone snickered. "If I were scared of sweat, I wouldn't come to a gym."

I giggled. "You're crazy, you know that?"

He grinned. "And you're beautiful when you smile, you know that?"

I smiled so hard it hurt my cheeks. "I appreciate that. Thank you."

He stood, setting me down onto my feet. "So, you hungry?"

I shrugged. "Yeah, I could eat."

He chuckled. "Well, go get yourself a shower, and you can meet me out front. Dinner's on me."

I pointed up at him as I backed away. "You better not follow me this time, either."

He growled lowly. "Now, that's just a challenge, gorgeous."

His tone shivered me to my core as I turned around and booked it for the door. Only a few minutes ago, my body felt like it couldn't go on. And within the span of being with Boone for only a little while, I felt ready to go a second round. Fuck the fact that neither of us had gotten a decent night's sleep since the beginning of the weekend. Whenever I was around Boone, I felt larger than life. I felt rejuvenated. I felt the dark parts of my soul slowly coming out to bask in his light for the first time since I had lost my brother.

I never wanted these feelings to end.

I rushed into the women's locker room and shed my clothes. I hopped into the quickest shower I'd ever taken in my life. And as I wrapped my towel around me, I stepped out, trying to hunt down my locker so I could get some fresh clothes on until I heard the locker room door open.

"I thought I already told you," I said with a giggle.

I heard Boone's footfalls stop behind me. "Ten bucks says I can get you off before they come looking for us."

I slowly turned around. "Oh, you are so on."

He charged my body, pressing me against the lockers as his lips crashed against mine. I groaned down the back of his throat as his hands gripped the towel away from my naked body, and I wanted nothing more than to enjoy him for the rest of the night. I jumped and wrapped my legs around him. He walked me around the corner to where the showers were before we found ourselves in a dry one with the curtain closed.

Then, he sank to his knees and slid my leg over his shoulder. "*Mmm*, I've been waiting years for this," he groaned.

His tongue pierced my folds, and my eyes rolled back. My hands flew into his soft, thick, brown tendrils, and I pulled him closer, feeling his tongue flatten against my clit. I bucked against the stubble of his face, feeling his hands gripping my thighs as I rocked against him. And as the heat in the pit of my gut started building, his name dripped from my lips.

"Boone. Oh, holy shit, Boone. Right there. Right there. Don't stop, please."

He growled against my pussy, and my body shivered. His tongue traced the tender outline of my most sensitive region, and my legs started quivering. I felt my juices dripping onto his face, marking him the way he had marked me. And as that coil tightened behind my abs, my nails raked against his scalp until his tongue threw me over the edge.

"Oh. My. Go— Boo–Boone— Oh you—"

My legs gave way, and he shot up, catching me before I hit the floor. I trembled in his arms as he held me close, smelling of my scent as he ran his fingers through my hair. We both slowly sank to the bottom of the shower, our bodies leaning against one another for support.

And as my heart fluttered a million miles a second, only one thought crossed my mind.

I think I'm falling in love with this man.

🏵 19 🏵

Boone

I *think I'm falling in love with this woman.*

The thought hit me like a ton of bricks, and all I could do was accept it. I'd never been left so helpless and so breathless after a few short experiences with a woman before. But dammit, Kate had worked herself beneath my skin in ways I'd never once fathomed in my entire life. I couldn't shake her. I mean, the way she felt, the way she spoke, the way she wrinkled her cute little nose every time she laughed... all of it culminated into this beautiful woman I got to enjoy and experience.

And fucking hell, I loved being inside of her.

That wasn't all of it, though. In fact, while sex usually dominated my world when it came to the opposite sex, it wasn't that way with Kate at all. I found myself becoming addicted to everything about her. The way she smelled and walked. The way she loved going to the gym and didn't give a shit about what she looked like while sweating.

And as we both sat at dinner with our drinks in our hands, that beautiful orgasmic flush was still apparent in her cheeks, even though it had been over an hour since our locker-room shower showdown.

I love that I can make her feel that way.

Kate whistled at me. "Hey, Boone. You gonna come back to earth anytime soon?"

I shook my head quickly and focused on her. "Sorry, your beauty is simply distracting."

She snorted. "Good one. But, I'm wondering how much of what I'm saying is actually registering."

I blinked. "Maybe not as much as you'd like."

She giggled. "I'd be offended if I didn't think you were so hot."

I winked at her. "You make me happy, so maybe that's what I'm thinking about. Ever think about that?"

But, her face fell flat. "Wait, really?"

"Really what?"

"I—I make you happy?"

I narrowed my eyes. "Is this a trick question? Or, are *you* really the one not paying attention?"

She still looked dumbfounded, though, so I leaned forward and nodded.

"Yes, Kate. You make me incredibly happy."

Then, she smiled, and it lit up her deep-emerald eyes in ways that made my heart flutter. "You make me happy, too. So happy that I can't even explain it sometimes."

I chuckled. "Really?"

She nodded. "Really."

"Even after all the shit, I pulled in high school?"

She snickered. "Yeah, believe it or not. Even after all of that shit, you pulled in high school."

My cheeks puffed out with my sigh. "Wow. That's—that's heavy stuff right there."

"I think it's a little more than that for me, though."

Wait. What? "Oh?"

She nodded. "Yeah."

I tilted my head to the side. "How so?"

She licked her lips. "I don't know. I guess I just—"

Jesus, is she going to say it? "Whatever it is, I hope you know that you can tell me."

Her gaze fell to her lap. "You just— You make me feel normal, you know?"

Oh. "Normal?"

She chewed on the inside of her cheek. "Yeah, normal. You know, a little less out of place down here in a town where I no longer have a family. You kind of make this place feel like home again."

Her words struck me to my core. "I'm really glad I can make you feel that way."

She smiled softly. "Me, too."

Dinner was pretty quiet after that point. I felt her stealing glances, and I sure as hell stole them back, but both of us focused a little too much on our food. And I understood. I got why we both did that. It seemed that we both had issues opening up to people, but little by little, we were peeling back each other's layers.

I simply hoped it never ended.

"Ready for a surprise?" I asked.

Kate wiped off her mouth. "What kind of surprise?"

I stood and offered her my hand. "How about you come with me so I can pay the bill, and then you can figure it out."

She smiled and took my hand. "Sounds like a plan, handsome."

I threaded our fingers together as my heart stopped in my chest. If I weren't careful, Kate would be the only fatal blow my heart needed. And while that wasn't a bad thing, I'd never been in this kind of territory with any other woman, and I wasn't sure what to do next. What I did know, however, was this—I wasn't ready for my evening to end with her yet.

After paying for dinner and escorting her back to my truck, I started meandering around town. We listened to music with our fingers intertwined and commented on things that had slowly changed around Conroe since our high school years. For instance, the high school had another trailer added into the mix for students being bussed in from other over-flowing larger cities around us. More money had been invested into the football field, so there were new paint lines on the grass for the first time in forever. Hell, we even took walks down memory lane, and she told me all about the ice cream parlor she and Sebastian used to go to every Monday after class.

She showed me her favorite coffee shop that her brother couldn't stand.

She even showed me where she had her first kiss...

... as well as the spot where Sebastian beat the kid's ass for kissing his sister.

I shrugged. "If I had a kid sister, I probably would've been similar."

She snickered. "Doesn't shock me one damn bit."

Not once did she ever let go of my hand.

However, after meandering around town, we found ourselves parked in front of a breathtaking flower garden that volunteer stay-at-home mothers in the Conroe area donated their time to keep up. In the summer and fall months, it was a communal garden where people could come and help cultivate foods that not only benefitted restaurants but our own tables. And during the transition months from winter on into spring, it was filled with all sorts of tulips and sunflowers and daisies and wildflowers.

And as we sat there, staring at the gorgeous expanse of colors stretched out before us beneath the moonlight, we watched lightning bugs dance around in the night air.

"Wanna catch some?" Kate asked.

I slowly looked over at her and grinned. "You read my mind, gorgeous."

The two of us slammed out of my truck and went dashing down the little cobblestone pathway. We ran through the flowers until it dumped us out into a small square block of grassy knoll that housed a gazebo and a couple of benches for people to sit. Lightning bugs lit up the world around us, casting a luscious hue against the petals of the flowers that kept catching my eye every time they flashed. But they had nothing on the radiant smile beaming from Kate's lips.

"I caught one!" she exclaimed.

I watched her unfurl her hands before the lightning bug lit up, flapped its wings, and took flight once more. Between her laughter, her smile, and my heart feeling fuller than it had in years, it felt like I had found my own slice of paradise.

Way to go, brother.

"Come on, Boone! There's more over here!" Kate exclaimed.

But, DeShawn's voice kept echoing off the corners of my mind.

I'm proud of you.

And you said you'd never find her.

Go get her, man. That's your world right there.

The idea that I might have actually fulfilled my promise to my guys seemed both insane and plausible. I jogged up to Kate, watching as she caught lightning bugs and released them with all the love and compassion the world had to offer bubbling behind her excited eyes. I couldn't help myself as I wrapped my arms around her and pulled her in for a kiss beneath the moonlit sky. And when her body pressed heatedly against my own, it breathed a renewed sense of life back into my soul.

I could love you for the rest of my life if you keep this cute shit up.

Kate gasped. "What did you just say?"

My eyes widened. "What?"

She blinked. "What?"

Holy fuck, did I say that out loud? "What's wrong?"

She took a step back from me. "Did you just—say that you love me?"

I'm a fucking idiot. "I—I just said—"

Kate turned away from me. "I think I should probably head home. It's getting late, and I'm starting to—"

I reached out for her. "Please, don't go." I gripped her arm and stopped her movements, but she didn't turn toward me. "I'm sorry. I never should have—."

She whipped around, causing my words to cease. "Please, don't ever apologize for something so beautiful that I can't say back. Okay? Because apologizing for it is even worse than not saying it at all."

I had no idea how to process any of that, and I didn't want to. I had already ruined an absolutely perfect moment, bringing us right back to square one.

Of course, I'd find a way to fuck it up. "Do you still want to go home?"

Kate nodded sadly. "Yeah. I think it's for the best."

I released her arm. "All right, let me get you home, then."

The truck ride was silent. Walking her up to her door was quiet. Watching her slip into her house without me killed me more than I wished to admit. I had this perfect woman right there in my grasp, and I had found a way to wreck it.

How many times would I have to break my promise to my buddies before I finally got things right?

Her door closed, and I stood there, wondering if I should have followed her. If I opened the door and demanded that we talk, would she take it well? Or would she slap me across the face? Then, it hit me.

We're still married.

"God*dammit!*" I roared. I spun around on my feet and slammed my palm against the railing of her porch. "Fuck!" I yelled.

"Hey!" a woman called out from afar.

I raised my hand. "Sorry! Sorry! Just—stubbed my toe."

I waved at Kate's neighbor, but she scowled at me before hurrying her children back into the house. Great. I wasn't even good enough for someone's fucking children to be around anymore. I shook my head and blazed a trail to my truck, slamming myself inside. I gritted my teeth. My breathing became ragged as anger swelled my chest. Long gone was the pride of flushing Kate's skin with an ethereal read. Long gone was the relaxing warmth of her touch against the palm of my hand. Long gone were the stolen kisses, the explosive intimacy, and the unfettered access to a body I wanted to worship every day for the rest of my life.

And after beating my fists against the steering wheel, I cranked the engine so I could head back home.

Still, with no end in sight as to our original issue of what the ever-blessed hell we were going to do about being married.

❈ 2 0 ❈

Kate

As I fell into my recliner in my living room, I leaned back. I stared up at the ceiling, feeling my tears drying against my cheeks as more slid down the side of my face. I felt the liquid gathering in my ears, but I didn't care. Nothing mattered after what happened last night.

There wasn't enough caffeine in the world to right my mind. And I knew because I was on my fourth cup of coffee, and I still felt disoriented. There wasn't enough makeup in the world to cover up how puffy and crazy my eyes looked after, crying to myself all through the night.

And when I reached into my bra, pulling out the dilapidated wedding ring, I eased it back onto my left-hand finger before bursting into sobs once more.

"Why am I so fucked up?" I asked through my tears.

Boone's words had been so genuine. So kind. So nurturing and caring and... and true. And fucking hell, my gut reaction was to run from it. To run from him. To run as far as I could so I didn't get attached to someone else, I'd ultimately lose. Sebastian's death had been enough for me, and I couldn't take loving someone else only to lose them for good.

Wait, when did I go from hating this boy to liking the man he had become?

I dug the heels of my hands into my eyes and tried to reset my brain. Everything felt so impossible and not at the same time. Yeah, Sebastian's death had really fucked me up. But, it shouldn't have screwed me over so much that I couldn't attempt a relationship with a man like Boone.

But, before I had the answer, a knock came at my front door.

I shot up from my chair and leaped to my feet. I raced toward the door, but I paused with my hand on the knob. Who in the world was bothering me in the middle of a supposed workday? I checked my cell phone in my pocket and saw that it was only ten-thirty in the morning.

Then, the knock happened again. "Delivery."

"Well, at least it isn't Boone," I murmured.

I opened the door and saw an older gentleman holding a massive teddy bear and a gift box along with a vase of yellow roses. I took everything out of his hands and thanked him, but he simply waved it away when I tried to tip him. I watched as he walked back to his delivery truck, his nose stuck in his phone as he climbed back in. Then, I kicked my front door closed and walked into the kitchen to set the presents down.

"Oh, Boone," I whispered.

I plucked the card from the holder in the beautiful-smelling roses but was hesitant to open it. I knew who this stuff was from, but I dreaded what was in that card. What if it was Boone telling me he loved me? Then, what? Or, worse. What if these were break-up flowers?

Are break-up flowers a thing?

My trembling fingertips slowly opened the letter before I slid the cardstock out of the small white envelope. On the front of the card, my name was written in calligraphy, and when I flipped the card over, something akin to relief flooded through my system. And with each passing read, I grew more and more relieved.

Kate,

Whenever you're ready, I'd like to bring food over so we can talk. I think that's what we need to do, just sit and talk. Let me know when you're free, even if it's not for months. Whenever you're ready to talk, so am I.

Boone

I set the note gingerly on the table and reached for the bear. The soft texture made me smile, and I cradled it closely before I turned my attention to the gift box. My heart started beating a million miles a second. If these weren't break-up flowers, then that gift could be anything. But, I decided to

place my nerves off to the side—along with the teddy bear—
and unwrap the present.

I took it apart, piece by piece until I slid the top off the
white box beneath the beautiful glittering wrapping paper.
And when I saw all of the fluffy stuffing inside of what looked
like clothing store packaging, I saw a white velvet square
sitting in the middle of it all with a little red bow on top of it.

It looks like a ring box.

My hand quivered as I picked up the smaller box. I placed
it in my palm and slowly cracked it open. And as I chanted,
"please don't be a ring" inside my head a million times, I was
pleasantly surprised at what I found.

"Wow," I whispered.

Against a white backdrop was a beautiful rose gold necklace with a rose-and-white-gold heart-shaped locket in the
middle of it. I lifted the glistening piece of jewelry out of the
box and dangled it in the air, studying it as a smile crossed my
face. It twirled slowly in midair, capturing the sunlight
streaming through my kitchen window before bouncing it
against the wall in all sorts of rainbow-like colors.

Then, I settled it into my palm and opened up the little
heart before the tears started flowing again.

"My God, Sebastian," I whispered.

Inside of the locket was a picture of my brother and me
from when we were little. To the left was us as children, with
our arms wrapped around each other, and to the right was a
picture of Sebastian and me the day I had graduated from
high school. Tears streaked my cheeks as I placed it around

my neck. I brought the images back to my face before closing the locket and tucking it into my cleavage to keep it safe and close to my heart.

For a split second, I wondered where the hell Boone had gotten those pictures. Then, I remembered what he did for a living and almost started laughing.

"You son of a bitch," I whispered with a smile on my face.

I raced up to my bedroom and stood in front of my dresser mirror. The necklace had little rings that enabled me to adjust how deeply the neck plunged against my chest. I tried it on every level, leaving myself some time to figure out which length I enjoyed the most. But, after deciding on hanging it around the middle of my neck, I played with the small heart and wondered what Boone was up to. So, I decided to get cleaned up and go see him at work.

It didn't take long for me to get ready, especially since my face's red puffiness cleared up with the cool shower I took. I slid into a basic pair of leggings and a nicer tunic before opting for some flats, then I scooped my things up and headed out the door. I raced over to where Boone worked— or where I figured he worked with the little bit of sleuthing I had done online—but when I pulled into the parking lot, I saw three separate cop cars sitting out front.

And all of the brothers were standing at the building's entrance.

At least I got the right place.

I fingered the necklace against my skin one last time before I slipped out of my car. I wasn't sure if this were a good time or not since I didn't know why the police were at Boone's company to begin with, but I figured if things felt off, I could always come back. I closed my car door behind me and slid my purse up my shoulder, my eyes darting around the small crowd that had gathered as I searched for Boone.

And when our eyes met, I watched his light up. "Hey, Boone!"

I waved at him, and my heart came alive at how big he smiled. All because of me. That smile, just because I decided to come to see him at work. The only other person I'd ever made smile that big—other than my friends from high school—was Sebastian. And to see that I could make Boone that happy as well warmed my soul. He broke away from the pack and started jogging toward me, meeting me halfway as we stood in the parking lot.

And as I gazed up into his gorgeous face, I couldn't help but smile.

You're in deep, girl.

Only this time, I wasn't as frightened as I had been last night.

21

Boone

I saw her the second she pulled up. I saw her car coming down the road, I saw her pull into the parking lot, and I saw her sitting there for a little bit before she stepped out. And when I saw that necklace glittering against her neck, I knew I had done well. I waffled around with the idea of sending her a gift, especially with how things went down last night. But, when I saw her smile as she met me in the middle of the parking lot, I knew I had done right by her, which is all I wanted to do.

"Hey, Boone!"

She waved at me, and I waved back before we came to stand in front of each other. And while this was probably the worst time she could have ever dropped in on me, I was still elated to see her. Part of me went to sleep last night believing I'd never see her again. Part of me really did think that when she had run away from me last night, she had run for good. I was so fucking happy I chose not to listen to that part of me this morning.

I couldn't stop smiling as she fingered the necklace. She held it up for me to see, and I reached down, cupping the back of it with my hand. Seeing her beaming with pride made me want to buy her more things. More jewelry. More flowers and presents and stuffed animals, just so I could keep her smiling for the rest of her life. That was what she deserved, too. She deserved someone to shower her with gifts. She deserved someone who loved her smile as much as I did.

And after settling the locket against her bare chest, my eyes found hers. "It looks good on you."

I expected her to say "thank you" or possibly nod in acknowledgment. But instead, she threw her arms around me and hugged me as close as she could. It shocked me to my core, but I sure as hell wasn't wasting the moment. So, I quickly wrapped my arms around her and pulled her tight against my body.

"I'm so sorry," she whispered.

I shook my head. "Don't be. All I can ask is that you be honest."

She sighed. "I never should've walked away from you last night."

"You did what you had to do. I'll never fault you for that."

She nuzzled into the crook of my neck. "You really mean that?"

She feels like home. "I never say anything I don't mean."

She kissed my neck softly. "Thank you."

I grinned. "I'm glad you're here."

"Boone?"

"Yeah?"

"I need to explain what happened last night."

I shook my head. "You don't have to explain anything you don't want—"

But, she interrupted me and started talking much too quickly. "I just don't want to lose someone else I love. I don't want to get attached to someone, and then something happen to them, and I never see them again. Losing Sebastian almost broke me. It marred me so badly that I had to completely switch careers. And losing someone else that I love like that is going to do me in for good. I know it will."

I froze at her words. "Love?" I felt her stiffen, but she didn't say anything. "Kate, look at me."

She hesitated, but she pulled away, and her eyes found mine. "Yeah?"

I gripped her chin with my fingertips. "Do you love me?"

She shook her head slowly. "I'm not there yet. Not where you are, anyway. But, I know I could be if we give it time."

I smiled softly. "Me, too."

"That's why I ran last night. I just—the idea of losing someone like that again makes me physically sick."

I nodded slowly. "Trust me, I understand that, too."

Her eyes grew somber. "I'm such an idiot. I'm so fucking sorry."

I cupped her cheek. "I swear to you, it's okay. No more apologizing, all right? I'm just glad you're here. It means I haven't lost you just yet."

Then, she nodded over my shoulder. "What's going on over there?"

I sighed and rolled my eyes. "Remember those red-flashing screens I was dealing with?"

"Yeah?"

"Well, they've come to a head."

She stepped out of my grasp, but her hand slid into mine. "Can you talk about it?"

I peered over my shoulder at my brothers. "It's all come out into the light now, so I suppose I can."

"All right, I'm all ears, handsome."

My heart fluttered at her words. "The flashing-red screens you bore witness to in Vegas was actually the second of two hacking attempts into our secure files."

Her eyes widened. "Wait. What?"

I threaded our fingers together. "Yep. Someone has been trying to hack our accounts for God-only-knows what purposes, and I was able to back-trace both attacks to the same IP address."

"Tell me you got the son of a bitch."

I snickered. "Something like that. In the beginning, we handed over whatever we knew to the police. And between my cybersecurity skills and their sleuthing skills, we were able to answer a few hard questions we had that no one seemed to have answers to."

She cocked her head. "So, who did it? Who's the hacker?"

I drew in a deep breath. "One of our investors on our board, Mr. Blanchard, has a daughter who invested some of their family's money into a rival petrol company. Mr. Blanchard used his daughter's name as a way to skirt around a clause in our board of investors contract that says he can't invest with any other rival companies so long as he's investing with ours."

She scoffed. "What a shitbag."

I chuckled. "Oh, it gets so much worse. As his daughter started learning the ropes, she started taking on a more 'hands-on' approach to what started out as a simple way to skirt the rules. And she became so involved with this rival company that she agreed to use her father's computer—who is *our* investor—in order to gain access to information that could put our rival company worlds above our own."

She blinked. "That sounds like some shit right out of a movie right there."

"You're telling me."

"I didn't actually realize this stuff happens in real life."

I shrugged. "Not too often, but it does."

She puffed her cheeks out with a sigh. "Well, at least you have answers and found the person responsible?"

I nodded. "That is a plus, yes."

She slipped her hand out of mine and started mindlessly

fiddling with her locket. "What will happen to this guy and his daughter now that they've been found out?"

I slid my hands into my pockets and grinned. "Well, the situation sucks, but it also convinced Will to agree to the plan."

"Uh... what plan?"

"My older brother, Wyatt, brought up the idea of buying out our board of investors and making our company a truly family-run company. And these shenanigans on Mr. Blanchard's part have convinced him to get on board."

She nudged me playfully. "I take it he was the last person you guys had to convince?"

I nodded. "Yep. And now that we're all on board, we can finally get the ball rolling with something we should have honestly done a long-ass time ago."

Her smile grew wide. "Sounds like we should celebrate, then."

And that's when Bart's voice sounded behind me. "I like the sound of that! Who's up for a party?"

Wyatt's voice popped up out of nowhere. "You know I'm always down for some mid-day fun. What did you guys have in mind?"

Someone patted me on the shoulder before I looked over and saw Ryan grinning at me. "And who is this beautiful little number you're chatting with over here?"

Kate giggled. "Hello, Ryan."

My brother paused. "Do we know each other?"

I gestured to my brother. "Ryan, this is Kate Riley. Kate, this is Ryan."

His jaw fell open. "Holy shit, *that* Kate Riley?"

Wyatt leaned against me. "Right? That's what I said."

Ryan leaned forward. "When did you say that?"

Wyatt leaned forward as well, talking like I wasn't sandwiched between the two of them. "This weekend. They ran off to Vegas together, and I'm supposed to act like I don't know shit about it."

I rolled my eyes. "Yeah, thanks for that, Wyatt."

He patted my back. "Anytime, brother. You know I always gotchu."

The guys chuckled before Bryce spoke. "What's that on your finger, Kate?"

My eyes fell to her hand before she quickly covered it up, and I felt my face pale. Hers reddened with shock, and I saw her arm muscles twitching beneath her skin. But, Will wrapped around behind her and chuckled.

"Whatever it is, she just slipped it into her pocket," he said.

"What?" Kate squealed. She whipped around and swatted at him, and I couldn't help but think about how well she already fit in with everyone.

"So, tell me," Wyatt said as he propped his arm against my shoulder, "you go to Vegas with some random girl you bullied in high school, you come back, she appears in the parking lot hugging on you and shit, and all of a sudden she has to work a ring off her finger?"

Will smiled. "Care to elaborate?"

"Nope," Kate said flatly.

Bryce eyed me carefully. "Everything go okay in Vegas?"

I shot him a look. "It's a long story, and we can talk about it later, all right?"

"Can I die now? Please?" Kate asked.

Bart slid his arm around her shoulders. "You can't die on us. We haven't even started the party yet!"

My brothers threw their fists into the air and yelled "yeah!" and as they did, I gazed deeply into Kate's eyes. Her cheeks were red with embarrassment, but she didn't seem as tense as she had last night. In fact, she seemed to be relaxing as my brothers started cheering on this party and throwing around all sorts of last-minute details for tonight.

"We gotta call Mom and Dad. They're gonna love this shit."

"Oh, beer. We need more beer for Bryce's garage fridge."

"Don't forget Dad's whiskey, either. He'll be pissed if you forget it."

"I've got steaks that have been marinating in the fridge unless we want to go out?"

I smiled. "Kate, you got any input on this party you've apparently started?"

She looked around at all of my brothers before her stare came back to mine. "Why waste a perfectly good buzz trying to grill food when we can have someone cook it for us."

Wyatt pointed at her. "I like her. Keep her around. Don't fuck it up, okay?"

I barked with laughter. "I'll try my best, you guys."

Bryce started jogging behind us. "I'll lock up the building really quickly."

Bart turned on his heels. "I'll make sure everyone is dismissed for a long weekend. I think we could all use it at this point."

Wyatt slid his hands into his pockets. "I need to grab some stuff from my office, then I'm good to go."

Ryan patted my shoulder. "You two talk about where you might wanna go because you know these guys will be up for whatever happens so long as there's booze."

Will chuckled as he nudged my shoulder, walking past me. "Just don't make it that damn taco hut again. I've had it twice this week, and I'm already over it."

I looked down at Kate. "What are you craving? Anything in particular?"

She considered my words before she licked her lips. "I want a slab of steak on top of a mile-high pile of alfredo pasta."

Ryan groaned. "Ugh, that sounds fantastic. And I know just where we can get it."

I smiled. "The steakhouse?"

He slapped my chest. "The fucking steakhouse, my man."

I nodded behind me. "Go tell everyone where we're congregating. Kate and I can head over there and snag a table at the back of the restaurant so we can really cause a ruckus."

Kate quirked an eyebrow. "Does this mean I'm going to be

babysitting a bunch of drunk guys? Because I enjoy throwing them back, too."

I winked at her. "No worries. I'll carry you out myself if you get sloppy on me."

She gasped playfully. "Why, I never! Boone Remington, a lady, never gets sloppy."

Unless it's my tongue between your thighs. "You sure about that?"

Ryan chuckled as he pulled away. "You two try not to jump each other's bones before we can eat. Save that shit for dessert."

I scoffed. "Such a prude, you are."

Kate snorted; she laughed so hard. "You guys are a hoot. This is gonna be a great lunch party."

And as Ryan walked away to go fill in the rest of the guys, I offered my arm to Kate. She accepted it without hesitation, and I escorted her to my truck before opening her door for her.

"So, wearing that ring just for shits and giggles?" I asked.

She climbed up and swatted at my chest, playfully. "So maybe I missed you. What's the harm in that?"

I missed you, too. "Nothing at all, beautiful. Nothing at all."

I closed her door and walked around the hood so I could climb behind the wheel of my vehicle. We started toward the restaurant, and I felt her hand effortlessly slide against my knee. I looked down at our connection—at her left hand seated against my right knee—and as I studied her ring finger during red lights, I saw the ring I'd get her one of these days.

A proper engagement ring fit for the queen she had become to me. I only hoped she kept me around long enough for me to show her that I was worth the risk of loss she feared so much.

Because she was definitely worth the risk for me.

22

Kate

"Hey, hey, hey," Ryan said as he snapped at Will, "pass the rolls. You've had four."

Will pulled the basket toward himself. "And I'm gonna have more, get your own."

"Will," Bryce warned.

The restaurant was an absolute madhouse, and yet I couldn't take my eyes off anything. When Boone said we needed a table for at least fifteen of us, I honestly thought he was joking. But, when all of the wives and a couple of their children started showing up, we ended up having to add four more spots to the massive table we had already booked.

And it was quickly filled with the sounds of a family.

I cuddled against Boone and watched, drinking it all in. It

had been so long since I'd experienced any sort of a family dynamic, and to be honest, a little bit of it was overwhelming. Kids were laughing and demanding fries with their chicken nuggets. Ryan and Will wouldn't stop fighting over rolls. Wyatt—for some reason—kept hogging all of the whipped butter. And I quickly found out that Bart had a very unhealthy obsession with sweet tea and lemonade mixed together...since he was on his fourth glass since he had arrived —twenty minutes ago.

"You okay?" Boone asked.

I looked up into his face and nodded. "Yeah, I'm okay."

"You sure? It's not too much? Because trust me, I'd understand if it was too much."

I smiled. "No. It's perfect. Thank you for bringing me."

He held me tight against his body. "I wouldn't want anyone else with me right now."

His words brought a light into my soul I had been missing ever since my brother had passed away. I nuzzled beneath his chin and closed my eyes, enjoying bits and pieces of conversations I kept picking up. I got to know some about their personalities and how they responded to certain events. I learned a bit about their sense of humor and what made them jive as a family unit.

"You guys missing someone?"

Everyone jumped up and screamed, "Hey!"

I almost leaped out of my chair. Boone kissed my temple, whispering sweet nothings into my ear as the table got up and rushed an older couple that had just walked in. I would never forget their faces, though. They'd always been prominent people in the community of Conroe.

When Boone's parents sat down in front of us, I sat up straight. But, I still felt Boone's hand lingering against my thigh.

"Kate, right?" his mother asked.

I nodded. "That's me."

She reached her hand over, and I took it. "My, my, you've really grown. You were only a junior in high school the last time I saw you."

His father's eyes grew somber. "I'm really sorry about Sebastian."

His mother squeezed my hand. "How are you holding up these days?"

Their kindness almost made me cry. "Some days are harder than others. But, I'm getting along better than I was."

She smiled kindly. "That's really good to hear."

Her father leaned over toward me. "Have you tried the filet mignon here? I don't care what anyone says. I've never had a steak like the way they do it here. I swear, they inject it with something that's probably illegal."

I giggled at his words as Boone moved his hand up my thigh and around to my spine. He massaged my lower back with his fingertips, and it took all I had not to start groaning at the table. His hands were pure heaven against my skin, even if my skin was clothed, and it made me want to whisper to him to meet me in his truck for a few minutes.

But, a woman's voice caught my ear. "So! What do you do for a living, Kate?"

Boone whispered into my ear, "That's Willow, Bryce's wife."

I nodded. "Willow, right?"

She smiled. "Yeah! That's me. And this is Sadie—"

The girl beside her waved. "Hi there."

"—and Ellie—"

A girl with what looked like soot running across her forehead nodded at me. "'Sup?"

"—and this is... well, I'm sure everyone else will introduce themselves eventually," Willow finished.

I giggled. "You guys have a massive family. Do you get together often like this?"

Sadie nodded. "Every Sunday for dinner."

Ellie shrugged. "Every once in a while, someone can't make it. You know, sick kid or sinuses or work or something like that. But, for the most part, yeah. It's every Sunday."

My eyebrows rose. "Wow. That's incredible."

Sadie reached across Willow and patted my arm. "What about you? Where's your family from?"

Boone leaned back down into my ear. "You don't have to answer something you don't want to."

But, I shrugged him off. "Uh, well... my family was never really close. I mean, I was close to my brother before he passed away, but I don't have any sort of contact with anyone else anymore."

Willow's eyes grew sad. "I'm sorry if we touched on a sensitive nerve or something."

I shook my head. "No, no. It's really okay. I mean, the details and stuff might not be table-appropriate, especially with children around, but you're good."

Sadie sighed. "Promise?"

I smiled. "I promise."

Ellie grinned at me. "So, you never did answer what you do for a living."

I gasped. "Oh! Sorry. I work at the gym up the road. I'm a full-time personal trainer, and I run some of their classes."

Boone chuckled. "I'm her most expensive customer."

I didn't miss a beat. "And the most annoying."

The girls fell apart in laughter, and I found myself giggling along with them. I tilted my head back and gazed up into Boone's eyes upside down and half-expected to find him upset with me. But instead, all he did was smile and nuzzle his nose against mine before the table came to a dead standstill.

"Uh oh," Boone murmured.

I quickly sat upright. "Is everything okay?"

I saw everyone staring at us, and I wondered what I had already fucked up.

"So, uh... are you two an item?" Will asked.

I looked over at Boone and found him studying me. "Well?"

Wyatt chuckled. "You mean, you don't know?"

I smirked. "Well?"

And when Boone shrugged, it made me smile. "I'm game if you are."

So, I decided to be playful about it, and I ran my hands down my body. "Oh, I'm very game if you think you can handle all of this."

The girls started cackling and high-fiving me while his brothers started patting him on the back. And as we stole glances at one another, my heart didn't feel nervous. My gut didn't feel as if it were going to be sick. In fact, I felt a sense of peace and calm overcome me that both enveloped me and caught me off-guard.

I was at peace whenever I was with Boone.

And I never wanted that to end.

Then, Bryce stood and raised his wine glass high in the air. "I'd like to make a toast!"

Everyone picked up their glasses and watched Bryce as he cleared his throat. "To the last of the Remington boys finally planting roots. May he not screw this up like he usually does."

"Here, here," his parents said in unison.

Our jaws dropped in shock as everyone tossed back their drinks, and then I doubled over with laughter. There was so much happiness inside of me and so much elation that needed to come out that the laughter was almost second-nature. I leaned against Boone and held my stomach. I forced my giggling to calm down, but I also had to roll my lips over my teeth to get it to stop. I felt so at home amongst all of these people, despite how overwhelming it felt at times.

And pretty soon, we were all talking and yelling over piping-hot food that touched down in front of us.

"Oh, Kate, the girls and I are having a sleepover at Willow's. You should totally come," Sadie said.

Ellie nodded. "Mhm, and make sure to bring a bathing suit as well."

Willow smiled. "We always seem to end up in the hot tub with margaritas and pizza."

I blinked. "Booze, bikinis, and bread? Oh, I'm so down."

I high-fived the girls and caught Boone stealing glances at me with a grin on his face. And I knew what he was thinking. I felt it in the way he softly caressed my back. He was happy at how well I got along with his family unit, and I was, too. Because I knew that sometimes, family situations like this were "make or break" for some couples trying to make things work. I was glad we wouldn't have to worry about that bullshit.

But, after four hours of eating, drinking, and laughing, the company card footed the bill, and we were on our way back to Boone's office building. I needed to pick up my car and run some errands, and I was sure Boone still had work that needed to be done, even though the weekend was technically upon us.

But, when he pulled into the parking space beside my car, I was hesitant to get out.

"What's got you all timid on me now?" he asked.

I looked over at him and sighed. "You know, after growing up in the foster care system with no one but my brother to look after me, and then losing him in the thick of it all, it was really nice to be part of a family dynamic again."

He cocked his body to face me. "Wait, you were in the foster care system?"

I nodded slowly. "Yeah. I don't talk about it much, but Sebastian and I were given up when we were pretty small."

He shook his head slowly. "I didn't know that. You always talked about your parents like—"

"Like they were my parents? Yeah, it's just not something people openly want to talk about. Especially with the kind of uncaring foster parents we had."

He took my hand in his. "I'm so fucking sorry, Kate."

I shrugged. "I'm not. Some people just get a bad roll of the dice. I know I did. But you can't let that define you, you know? I can't let it be the only thing about me that's interesting."

He snickered. "You're an incredible fucking woman. I hope you know that."

I smiled. "You make me feel like one. Does that count?"

He leaned a little bit closer to me. "It'll do for now. But, we really need to work on that self-esteem of yours a bit."

I mocked his movements, leaning in so close I could feel his breath against my lips. "I do have confidence that I could whoop your ass in the gym any day, though."

His nose nuzzled mine softly. "Sounds like a challenge to me."

I love this man.

I didn't have the guts to say it out loud at that moment,

but when Boone's lips captured my own, and he pulled me into his lap? My heart preached a truth it had known for a few days now. I threaded my arms around his neck and let our tongues intertwine, giving in to the heat and the pull I'd felt in my gut ever since I had pulled into the parking lot four hours or so ago. I leaned against him, deepening our kiss as his hand threaded its way through my hair. And as I sat against him, I knew what I had to do.

I had to make sure I did whatever it took to keep this man in my life—for good.

23

Boone

"That'll be $102.42, sir."

I handed the woman my debit card. "Thank you very much."

"Is there anything else we can get for you before we check you out?"

I blinked. "Actually, do you guys have any sort of... massage oil or anything?"

The woman grinned before she dipped down and resurfaced with a small bottle of clear gel wrapped in an outer coating of red and white. "No charge. It's a sample. And if you like it? You can always come back and get a regular-sized bottle. They're only ten or so bucks a pop."

I grinned. "Good to know, thank you. I appreciate that."

I had been aching for days to whisk Kate away on a romantic date that would blow her mind. So, I had taken my entire Saturday and gone shopping. Not only did I pick out a new suit for myself to be rush-tailored for the evening, but I made special reservations at this great Italian place, complete with a private room and a menu procured only for us. I went and picked out a dress that I knew would look phenomenal on her and found a matching set of heels that would make any woman melt in her panties. And after paying for the slinky little lingerie number that I hoped she would elect to wear beneath the outfit, I headed out of the store, ready to drop off my presents at the gym.

With the gift bags in the backseat ready to be delivered, I pulled up to Kate's place of work. I knew she had to work a half-day today, but I wanted to catch her before she went on her mini-break. I strutted my shit through the gym and made my way into the weight room, and I found her helping some pimply teenager figure out the weight machines. So, I waited until she was done before I caught her attention.

"Kate!" I exclaimed.

She whipped around and smiled. "Boone! She rushed up to me and hugged me before even realizing I was carrying bags. "What in the world is all of this?" she asked.

I handed them to her. "For you. I'll see you at seven."

She furrowed her brow. "Wait. Wh—what is this, though?"

I winked at her as I walked backward. "And don't be late. Seven o'clock sharp, all right?"

"Oh—uh—yeah—but—but what are these things?"

I walked out of the gym without answering her questions and smiled to myself. Now, it was time for me to go home and prepare. I wanted a nice, clean-shaven face for the evening. I wanted to get a fresh haircut as well. So, after picking up my suit, I pampered myself with a manicure, a facial, a nice shave, and a trim before I went home to slip into my suit. "Oh, hell yeah, brother," I murmured to myself.

I modeled my pin-striped, navy-blue suit in the mirror, tailored specifically for my body. The matching navy-blue, button-up shirt beneath the suit coat didn't look like much, but when paired with a crisp white skinny tie, the damn thing popped and sizzled like no suit I'd ever worn before. It cost me a pretty penny, but Kate was completely worth it.

Then, I headed on to the restaurant.

"Mr. Remington! We are so glad you arrived. We're finalizing the drink menu, and we were wondering—"

I held up my hand. "I know what you're thinking, and the answer is 'no.' I know you guys specialize in wines, but my woman and I are solely beer drinkers. That's all I want on the drink menu tonight."

I met with the chef himself, and we went over the menu. I tweaked and changed a couple of things, but I also slipped him a Benjamin for his troubles. I knew that any last-minute tweaks to the menu they had procured for me would require a quick shift and a lot of work, and I wanted them to know that their work was appreciated. Plus, I wanted to light a fire under their asses to help me get everything perfect for Kate.

My next stop was the hotel. I did myself in a bit in Vegas

by going with what I thought was the nicest penthouse suite
the Strip had to offer. But, the hotel suite I had rented this
evening for us was right at the top and had a private balcony
overlooking the whole of Conroe, which was just as romantic,
in my opinion.

"Let's see, did they get everything I asked?" I murmured
to myself.

I checked the mini-bar and smiled when I saw it was
stocked with tequila and whiskey. I double-check the bedside
tables to ensure that I had brought over the lotions and
massage oil I wanted us to go through during our two-night
stay in our very own private room. I laid out some rose petals
in the bathroom leading to the jetted tub that could easily fit
the both of us, and I rearranged the bubble bath soaps and
bath bombs one last time before setting a bottle of cham-
pagne in a frozen bucket of ice.

Then, after positioning two crystal glasses on either side
of the bucket, I raced off to pick up Kate.

Now, I knew what Kate was wearing. I had picked out her
outfit, after all. But, when I knocked on her door, and she
slowly opened it, I wanted to throw all of our dinner plans out
the window and take her right on her fucking porch.

"Shit," I whispered.

Her eyes slowly ran down my body. "Holy hell, Boone.
How much did that suit cost you?"

I almost had to scrape my jaw off the concrete. "You look
—dear God, Kate, you look fantastic."

"Wow, don't sound so shocked."

Her voice snapped me out of my trance. "I just thought—"

She giggled and took my hand as she stepped outside. "I'm just playing with you. I'm really glad you like it, though."

I kissed her forehead. "I love it. Especially on you."

She giggled again, and it filled me with such pride and happiness. I thought I was going to burst out of my damn suit. The navy-blue dress fell just barely off her shoulders before cinching in at the waist and softly fluttering outward down past her knees. The shimmering fabric reminded me of the stars twinkling in the night sky when we were catching lightning bugs in the flower fields. And I knew the second I laid my eyes on that dress that it was perfect for Kate.

But, the way she filled it out with her curves left me salivating as we climbed into my truck.

I really do love this woman.

I held her hand the entire way to the restaurant, and the thought kept rushing through my head. But, the more it rushed and ran rampant, the more comfortable I grew with it. Kate was—by far—the most beautiful woman on this planet. But, she was so much more than that.

She was strong.

Resilient.

Intelligent.

Faithful.

Funny.

Ridiculous in all the right ways.

She was my puzzle piece, and I needed tonight to go perfectly because I had a question I wanted to ask her.

"Man, you can really wear a suit, you know that?" Kate asked.

I pulled into the restaurant parking lot. "Trust me, I'm over here trying to concentrate on the road, and I can't take my eyes off my own reflection."

She barked with laughter. "But for real, that suit would look fantastic on my floor."

I growled. "I love a good outfit that matches a nice floor."

The look in her eye as I helped her out of the truck told me she wanted to forgo dinner altogether. But, we had a lot we still needed to talk about. And there was still the issue of that pesky question I wanted to ask her that had been tumbling around in my mind for days. So, I escorted her inside on my arm before pulling out her chair at our private table in the back.

We placed our orders for food and drinks before we were truly left alone. And when Kate's gaze met my stare, I knew she was the one.

She was the one I wanted to spend the rest of my life with.

Dinner was filled with laughter and excitement. Our feet tangled up with each other's beneath the tablecloth as round after round of food came out for us. We went down the menu, trying out all of the beers and staving off an unhealthy buzz with just enough food to keep us upright. And after laughing over dinner for almost three fucking hours, I felt well enough to drive us to the hotel.

When we walked through the threshold, though, Kate

slowly turned to face me. "Is this for tonight? For us?" she asked breathlessly.

I led her into the room as the door softly closed behind us. "Well, I booked it for two nights, but I could technically book it out for two weeks if you wanted me to."

"Oh, Boone." She threw her arms around me, and I caught her mid-stride.

I wrapped my hands around her wrists and pinned them behind her as I crashed my mouth against her own. I bent her backward, holding her close to me as I pinned her hands to the small of her back. And as she groaned down the back of my throat, I let my tongue slide over the roof of her mouth.

She just looked so good in a grand, plush room that I couldn't help myself.

"Take me," she whispered against my lips.

I growled. "Let's see how my suit looks on this floor, then."

Gone was the question I wanted to ask. Gone were the conversations we needed to have. And instead, I enveloped Kate with my arms as she surrounded me with her warmth. We stumbled over to the bed, toeing off our shoes, and collapsing onto the mattress. She ripped my belt from its loops and threw it onto the floor, her fingers trembling as she tried to get me out of my clothes. We tossed and turned, stripping one another until there was only air separating the two of us.

And as I hovered over her, I watched her fingertips trace some of my tattoos.

"Wow," she whispered.

While she studied my ink, I studied her eyes. I thought about how beautiful it would be to have an accent wall in one of our rooms that matched the color of her irises. I thought about how beautiful a bedspread with an accent color of strawberry blonde might look in a nursery for one of our children one day, and that's when I knew.

That's when I knew I wanted to stay married to this woman.

"Kate," I murmured.

Her eyes met mine. "Your tattoos are incredibly intricate. Did they hurt?"

I slid beside her and shrugged. "Not particularly. They were a form of therapy for me, to be honest."

She continued sliding her fingertips along the lines. "Will you tell me their stories someday?"

I thought about the beautiful house I'd build for her. Built on the stories of our pasts in order to create a better future for ourselves. I thought about those floor-to-ceiling windows back in Vegas that had framed her body so well. I thought about how many times I'd fuck her against them if I lined our room with those windows.

"Yeah," I said with a kiss to her forehead, "someday I'll tell you all of them. How's that sound?"

She smiled up at me. "I've never felt more wanted or more cherished in all my life, Boone Remington. Thank you for what you've given me."

I took her hand and stopped its tracing, only to press her

palm against my heart. "And thank you for giving me peace, Kate Riley."

As we gazed into each other's eyes, lying naked in bed with one another, I knew I wanted to feel this way for the rest of my life. I wanted to wake up to this woman, make love to this woman, and live a life with this woman until we were old and gray and ready for our time to come.

"I love you, Kate," I murmured, without an ounce of fear welling in my body.

And when her eyes watered over, she captured my lips before murmuring those five beautiful words against my lips. "I love you, too, Boone."

Then, I captured her lips and raised us both up before I gathered her into my arms, determined to make love to her the way I should have back in Vegas.

❧ 24 ❧

Kate

The second I felt my back pressed against the cold glass, I gasped. But, my lips weren't alone for long before Boone's tongue filled me with warmth. I moaned as I slid my hands through his hair, clinging to him as my legs locked around his waist. I needed him. All of him. For the first time since losing my foundation, I felt steady again. And I felt that way because Boone had somehow become my rock.

"Oh, shit," he groaned.

I reached between us. "Now. Please. I need you now."

I stroked his cock before he reared back, and then my fingers parted my pussy lips just for him. And when he inched his way inside my body, he pinned my wrists above my head. I pressed against the glass as he kissed down my neck, nipping and sucking his way down my skin. And as I bucked ravenously against him, his tightly-wound curls raked against my clit, sending me into a spiraling, wet frenzy of lust.

"Oh, fuck. Just like that."

Boone planted his face between my tits. "Jesus Christ, I love you so much. How is that possible?"

I gripped his hair and hung on for the ride. "Don't question. Just do. I love you. I love you so much."

His breath panted against my cleavage. I felt his cock swelling against my walls. My fingertips slid along his scalp, shivering him from head to toe as goose bumps broke out along his skin. I lost myself in him. In the sounds and smells and sensations, he spread throughout my limbs.

And as our bodies rocked together, chasing a high we both desperately wanted, I unraveled against him as I cried out his name to the heavens. "Boone, yes!"

He grunted. "Shit, Kate. Just like that. Squeeze me. Oh, fuck. You're perfect—for—me."

I felt his hot threads of arousal coating me as I collapsed against his body. His hands planted against the window he had me pinned to, our bodies already fogging up whatever view people thought they might have of us. We both sank to the floor, tangled up in one another as we panted for air.

And after his cock slid from between my legs, the gush I felt reminded me of the love we had just made.

The love I had finally found.

The love I hoped never left me ever again.

My eyes started fluttering closed, and I didn't remember much after that. And when light blanketed my face the next morning, my eyes parted slowly, and I found Boone snoring softly next to me. My body ached in the best of ways. I sighed as I shuffled around, trying to get out of the tangled mess I weaved with the blankets around my legs.

Then, I scooted over and laid against Boone's pillow as he continued to snooze beside me.

I have the best husband ever.

I had every intention of talking with him about it last night. But, after everything we'd been through in such a short amount of time, and after our mutual feelings had been proclaimed, I wondered if it was something we actually didn't need to rectify. I mean, we loved one another. We enjoyed being around one another. So, why didn't we just keep trucking along like we were and not bother with doing anything about our Vegas marriage? Maybe things might turn out well for us if we simply let it be.

My eyes ran along the expanse of his body that I could see, and I saw little marks I had left behind with my nails. I clapped my hand over my mouth and stifled my giggles, hoping I didn't wake him up. He needed his beauty sleep, after all, if he was going to fuck me like that again before we went to get breakfast. And I sincerely hoped he was my morning dose of caffeine before we rolled out of bed to get food.

"You'd like him now, Sebastian," I whispered.

I felt Boone's hand slide against my bare hip as he cracked open an eye. "I know I'd like him now, too."

I giggled and kissed his lips softly. "Morning, sneaky snake."

He grinned. "Morning, fartface."

I blinked. "Well, that's not very nice."

He slid his hand up to my waist. "It is when you hear some of the doozies I caught on video record."

"Wait, what?"

He chuckled. "You fart in your sleep. And you really rip some good ones."

I pushed his chest. "You're a jerk. Did you really record me farting while I was sleeping?"

He grinned. "And if I did?"

I playfully glared at him. "You better lock the door when you poop now because if you don't, I'll bust in on you and record you mid-shit."

He acted like he was shocked. "You wouldn't dare."

I bumped his nose with my finger. "You. Just. Wait. Handsome."

I moved my finger and kissed the tip of his nose, but he moved at the last second and captured my lips. Our sleepy tongues fell together before he slowly rolled me over, his thick morning wood pressed against my stomach. I spread my legs for him, and I wrapped my arms around his back. His thickened girth slid against my pussy lips, teasing my sensitive clit as he stared down at me from his perched peak.

"Good morning, beautiful."

I raised up and captured his lips before I settled back against my pillow. "Morning, sexy."

He dipped down and kissed my neck. "Know what I need this morning?"

"*Mmm*, what?"

He wrapped his lips around my puckered peak. "You."

He slid effortlessly into me, and we lost ourselves in one another again. We rolled around, taking each other in positions I'd never once tried out before. We sweated together and panted together. I rode his cock before he flipped me over and pounded into me from behind. I came so many times I lost count. By the time I was about to beg for mercy, we both fell over the edge together before we collapsed against the mattress, sweaty and spent from our morning breakfast.

"Holy fuck," he groaned.

I puffed my cheeks out with a sigh. "You uh... you really know how to sling that thing around."

He rolled over and tossed his arm over my waist. "Ready for another nap?"

I giggled. "Only if you promise me two meals made of actual food when we get up. Because when I get up, I'm going to be starving."

He stretched his arm out to the side. "Hold on, I can fix that real quick."

He called down to the kitchen and placed a massive order for food and drinks to be delivered to our room in three hours. Then, the two of us fell asleep, wrapped up in one another. We woke up with enough time to take a shower together, and for the first time in my life, I had someone wash my hair for me.

Wash my body for me.

Condition my hair for me.

Hell, even put lotion all over my skin after I got out and dried off.

Boone pampered me from head to toe, and I felt like a queen when our food finally arrived.

"Mind if I put on one of your shirts? I didn't bring any clothes with me," I said.

Boone pulled his boxers on. "I don't care what you wear. You can stay naked for all I care."

I slid into his button-front shirt. "This looks comfy, though. *And* I was right."

I turned around and found Boone eyeing me hotly, but I simply wiggled my finger at him before heading out toward our meal. We pulled the rolling tray stacked with things right in front of us, and I turned on the television, flipping through channels until we found something we wanted to watch. We picked at our food and sipped our drinks, then Boone got up and grabbed us a couple of beers from a mini-bar I didn't even notice last night.

And as we cuddled together, with full stomachs and full hearts, my world finally felt whole again.

I could do this for the rest of my life.

Night slowly fell around us, and the sunlight streaming through the windows was quickly replaced with moonlight.

We spent the day sipping on beer and eating while lounging around half-clothed. It was a first for me since I had worked my entire life essentially. So, to have a lazy day that didn't somehow count against me was new and foreign, and oh, so wonderful.

"I don't know what you've done to me, but don't stop."

Boone's words echoed off the corners of my mind as I laid my head on his chest, listening to his heartbeat. "Trust me, I don't intend to. Because you've done the same to me, too."

He played with my hair. "Do you regret anything that's happened so far?"

I shuffled around and laid my head in his lap, gazing up into his face. "What do you mean?"

"I mean... us, doing this thing we're doing. Working out together. Vegas..."

I knew what he was getting at, and I smiled up at him. "No."

He looked down at me in shock. "No?"

I shook my head. "No."

"Not even Vegas?"

I reached up and cupped his cheek. "Especially not Vegas."

He nuzzled against my palm. "Me, either. Have I told you lately that I love you, Kate?"

My smile grew so big it hurt my whole face. "No. Have I told you lately that I love you, Boone?"

His smile matched my own. "I hope you don't ever stop saying it."

I smoothed my thumb against the stubble on his cheek. "I don't plan on it. You?"

"Never. I'll never stop saying it."

"Good."

And as he gathered me into his arms, bringing my lips to his for a kiss, only one thought crossed my mind—a thought that changed the course of my history, my emotions, my memories, and my world.

I finally found my life again.

A life I deserved with the most unexpected person I thought I'd deserve it with. I had found my peace inside of the man who had grown from the boy who had tortured me in high school. I had found a family again in the man who I had judged way too harshly in the beginning. And as I sat upright in his lap, twisting and turning so I straddled him, I cupped his cheeks and gazed into his eyes.

"I'll never let you go," I whispered. "Just like you'll never let me go."

Then, Boone gripped my ass cheeks, stood up, and walked me back over to the bed, where we made love to one another for the rest of our last night at the hotel.

EPILOGUE

Boone
Nine Months Later

Wyatt cleared his throat as he stood up. "Can I have everyone's attention, please?"

I chuckled and leaned over into Kate's ear. "When does he not want our attention?"

"I heard that," he said flatly.

Kate giggled. "Yeah, he heard that."

Wyatt slid his hand into his pocket as the Sunday dinner table at Rocking R Ranch went quiet. "I just want to take a second and thank each and every one of you for the hand you played in all of this over the last nine months. It's been exhausting, arduous, and I know sometimes it felt like we wouldn't actually pull it off. But, I'm here to announce that I got the paperwork in the mail."

All of us perked up as he set down his glass and pulled a rolled-up stack of papers from the inside of his suit coat.

"Is that what I think it is?" Ryan asked.

Wyatt unraveled them and started handing them out. "I got copies for each household, but let me know if you'd like more than one."

The guys and I clamored for our papers before Kate pulled me back into my seat.

"Holy shit," she whispered.

I kissed her temple. "We did it, babe. Holy fuck, we did it."

Wyatt nodded. "That's right, Boone. We did it. We've rebranded as Remington Petrol, and each brother—including our father, too—owns an equal portion in the company."

"It's about damn time, too!" Dad exclaimed.

"Here, here!" I said as I raised my glass.

"Here, here!" everyone else exclaimed.

We all clinked glasses and celebrated a moment that was a long time in the making. And now, we understood why Wyatt had wanted to host Sunday dinner this week. I read over the paperwork I never thought we'd finally get, and as I sipped my beer, I felt Kate stand up next to me.

But, when I looked up at what she was doing, never in my wildest dreams had I ever seen a more perfect sight.

I watched Sadie slip her and Will's newest addition to their family into Kate's arms. She stepped away from her chair, bouncing the sweet little one-month-old baby as she cooed and talked softly to the sweet little boy. Sadie and Will stood like two proud, tired-as-fuck parents, and before I could help myself, the words came flying out.

"If you guys ever need a babysitter, let us know."

Kate nodded. "Yes, please. We'd be more than happy to watch this cute little boy for an evening so you guys can get away."

Will chuckled. "Does that offer include the twins, too?"

Kate whipped her head up and nodded. "Oh, you know it does."

I cracked my knuckles. "Just know that I want to be the fun uncle. So, they'll probably eat everything they're not supposed to."

Kate whispered loud enough for me to hear, "Don't worry, I'll make sure none of that happens."

As I watched her play with and kiss those chunky baby cheeks, I started thinking about the children we'd eventually have one day. The thought made me smile, seeing Kate walking around, swollen with my seed. Watching her chase around little ones while I cooked dinner before we both did the dishes together and tackled bedtime one at a time.

Then, Bart nudged me. "What are you cheesing about over here, huh?"

I sighed. "Just—everything."

Kate handed Sadie their baby boy, but not before she kissed his precious little forehead. And when she turned back to me with those twinkling eyes of hers, I couldn't resist it a second longer. I stood to my feet as that tiny box sizzled a hole against my outer thigh. I scooted my chair in and offered my hand, helping Kate back down into her chair.

But, instead of sitting back down, I slipped my hand into my pocket before hiding the little box in my palm.

"Babe, everything okay?" Kate asked.

The table slowly fell silent as I drew in a deep breath. "Everything is perfect, sweetheart. Well, almost at least."

Her eyebrows rose. "Oh? Is there something wrong?"

"Actually, now that you mention it, there is."

As Kate studied my face, I acted as if I were about to sit back down in my chair. But, at the last second, I slipped to my knee in front of her. The girls squealed with shock, and my mother gasped so hard I thought she was going to inhale her own damn teeth. And when I felt one of my brothers pat me on the back, I cracked the box open.

Revealing the ring I had painstakingly designed for the love of my life over the course of the past three months.

"Oh, Boone," Kate whispered.

I chuckled. "You remember a few months back when we figured out that a 'certificate of marriage' isn't the same as a 'marriage certificate'?"

Her hands flew to her mouth, and she nodded. "Yes."

"And do you remember when I asked you how it made you feel?"

She nodded as her hands slipped into her lap. "Yes."

"You remember how you told me you were actually okay with it?"

"Yes, Boone."

I smiled. "I know you were lying through your teeth. So, before I launch into my spiel, I'd like to know how that actually made you feel."

Her eyes danced around my face before she swallowed hard. "I was disappointed."

I took her left hand in my own. "So was I. And that's what's wrong, Kate. What's wrong is that we were always destined to be together in the best of ways, but life always seems to find a way to twist things around for us. No more, though. It's completely unacceptable, and it's time for me to make it right. Hell, for us to make it right."

She nodded. "Yes, Boone."

I smiled as the beautiful emerald ring that shimmered like her eyes started reflecting off Wyatt's dining room walls. "We've always been drawn to one another. We've always been on the same path, even if we didn't want to admit it. But, it used to be through hate. And now, we're drawn together in love. In the way that we should have been drawn together had I not been such a jackass in high school. Through shared circumstances and shared pain and shared loss, I've found my person. My puzzle piece. The woman who completes me in this life. And I can't go another second without this travesty being right."

She leaned forward and cupped my cheeks. "Ask me, Boone, and you realize that I've already answered."

Tears rushed my eyes. "Kate Riley, I can't go another day

without being able to call you my wife again. Will you marry me?"

She stroked her thumbs against my cheeks. "Yes, Boone. I'll marry you. But, can I admit something?"

I sniffled. "Anything, my love."

Her forehead pressed against mine. "I never stopped thinking I was married to you."

And at her words, a tear slid down my cheek. "Neither did I, beautiful. Neither did I."

Bryce murmured behind us somewhere. "Did he just say, again?"

I heard a thwap and figured Willow had slapped him, and it only served to make the moment even better. Why? Well, because Vegas was our little secret. Our little moment of unadulterated, unjudged bliss that had brought us closer together than we could have ever expected.

And in some ways, I wanted it to stay like that forever.

A story of our love that only we knew.

"Dammit, kiss me and put that ring on my finger already," Kate murmured.

Her lips crashed against mine, and I stood, taking her with me as my arms blanketed her back. My tongue slid to the back of her throat, encompassing her and tasting her as I bent her backward. Everyone at the table stood up and cheered. Dad whistled through his teeth while Mom pumped her fist in the air, clapping the hardest out of everyone.

And when we both came up for air, I slipped that ring out

of the box and onto her finger, watching as it nestled perfectly against the skin.

"So," Ryan said as he patted my back, "I guess Vegas was more than meets the eye?"

Wyatt gripped my shoulder. "I mean, I knew you had secrets, but come on. Really? You left us out of that kind of juicy story?"

"It hurts, man. It really hurts," Ryan said.

I chuckled. "Ah, you'll get over it in time, I'm sure. And think of it this way. Now, Kate has a wedding ring fit for the queen she is."

"Oh, yes, I do," Kate said. "Willow!"

"Yeah?"

She lifted her hand into the air. "Come here. You guys gotta look at this sucker!"

The girls shoved their way through the throng of family members before they whisked Kate away, and I watched as happiness filtered up and down her entire body. She had changed before my very eyes, going from the angry woman I had run into at the gym and becoming the happy, bubbly, beautiful woman I had come to love. The girls ogled over the ring as she wiggled it around on her finger, and soon the camera phones were out to take pictures and tell the world that we had found one another again—the girl I never could take my eyes off of in high school.

"How does it feel?" Bryce asked.

Bart nodded as he walked up. "Yeah. Marriage is a pretty big step. You sure you're ready for it?"

Bryce smirked as he stood in front of me. "I think he's been ready for longer than he's been letting on. Haven't you?"

I'm proud of you, man. Way to go.

DeShawn's voice echoed off the corners of my mind, and whatever hesitation I might have possibly felt melted away. I gazed upon the rest of my life: my family, gathered around a Sunday dinner table with kids running around, my parents watching and laughing, and the love of my life giggling with the girls we had all managed to trick into loving us. We were a motley crew, this family unit. My brothers and half-brothers, all in business with one another. Our riches, climbing the charts as we took down our competition, one by one.

Our families, growing with children that would carry on our legacy far after we were gone.

"They'd be proud of you," Ryan said. "All of them."

Bryce nodded. "Yeah, they really would be."

Will snickered. "They'd love Kate, too. I mean, a woman who can keep up with your sense of humor? Shit, that's a world wonder right there."

I smiled and waved at Kate as our eyes met. "Don't I fucking know it?"

She waved back before flashing me the ring, and the happiness that sparkled in her eyes made me excited for what was to come. We had already planned the house we were going to build on the family's Rocking R Ranch. All we had to do was pick a start date. And in the meantime, hopping from her place to mine whenever we felt like it worked for us just fine. After all, we had the rest of our lives to enjoy living together. We had the rest of our lives to plant roots and make the house we'd build a home. We had all the time in the world to be exactly what we were destined to be.

"Come here, big guy," Kate said.

My brothers chuckled and patted my shoulders before congratulating us one last time. Then, I wrapped my beautiful fiancée up in my arms and let my lips fall against hers.

"Mmm, hey there, pretty girl."

She giggled against my lips. "How's that food settling? I know you were complaining a bit about a rough stomach this morning."

I shrugged. "Just needed to take a nice poop."

She wrinkled her nose. "Eww. Gross."

"Hey, it's no grosser than the craziness you dropped a couple of days ago. Your apartment still smells from it."

She balked. "It does not!"

I kissed the tip of her nose. "It's okay, though. I like your smelly midnight farts."

"Boone!"

"Well, I do!"

The family started laughing, and I drew Kate close to me. At first, she refused to kiss me, but enough nuzzling of my nose against her jawline coaxed her lips in my direction. I captured them fiercely, proclaiming how much I loved her with my tongue as I slid it over the roof of her mouth.

And as she melted against me, I felt the sudden urge to have another stomachache just so we could leave.

"They'd like you, you know," I murmured.

Kate pulled back softly. "What was that?"

I walked her away from the loud, crowded dinner table before we found ourselves in Wyatt's messy kitchen. "I said they'd like you."

It took her a second to register it. But, when she did, she smiled. "You think so?"

I tucked a strand of hair behind her ear. "I know so."

"Will you tell me about them someday? About the guys, you served with?"

I nodded. "Someday, yes. I'll tell you all about them. Just like I've told you about my tattoos."

She kissed my chest. "Do you feel like you did it?"

I paused. "Did what?"

She peeked up at me from beyond her eyelashes. "Your promise. Do you feel like you've kept your promise to them?"

I didn't hesitate. "Yeah. I do."

Not only had I upheld my promise to my buddies, but I had also upheld a promise to myself. A promise to live better and be better and do better in the eyes of my community. I fulfilled a promise to find my path in life, even if it set me at odds with the rest of the world. I promised to live my life in a way that honored those that weren't alive to do it for themselves.

And I could finally look in the mirror and tell myself that I had done it.

We did it, boys.

DeShawn's voice echoed back to me as if he were standing

right there. No, Boone. You did it. Just like I always knew you could.

"You okay?" Kate asked.

I felt her brush a tear away, and I snickered. "I'm perfect. I've never been so okay in all my life. And that's thanks to you."

She slid her arms around my waist. "Well, I'm sure owning a seventh of the third-largest oil company in the entire country doesn't hurt, too."

I chuckled as I ran my fingers through her hair. "No, that doesn't hurt, either."

"Just make sure you can take time off for our honeymoon. I'm expecting two full weeks with you without your laptops."

I gasped playfully. "Without my laptops? Whatever shall I do?"

She stood onto her tiptoes and pressed her lips to my ear. "Me, Boone. That's what you'll be doing."

I turned my head and captured her lips before I growled down the back of her throat. I leaned against the kitchen counter, feeling her pressing against me as her wondrous curves cloaked me away from the rest of the world. I tasted her love. I felt her happiness. I shared her excitement about what was to come. But, above all else, I felt the mutual respect we finally had for one another radiating between us as our tongues danced a familiar waltz they both had learned over the past few months.

And with God as my witness, I knew I'd never do a thing to compromise the life I had carved out for myself, if anything because Kate had become the most important person in my life to me. Something I wouldn't trade for anything in the world, even though it took me a while to morph into the man she deserved in her life. The man she needed. The man she had prayed for at night while lying in bed, wondering if anyone would have mercy on her.

"So long as I live, Kate, you'll never hurt another day in your life," I whispered.

She giggled softly. "Took the words right out of my mouth, big boy."

Together, forever.

At last.

Made in the USA
Monee, IL
24 June 2022